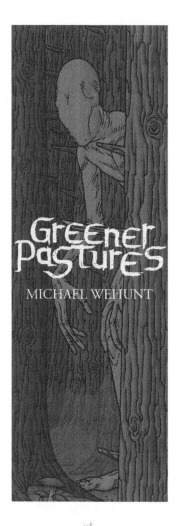

Greener Pastures

MICHAEL WEHUNT

Massachusetts • Pennsylvania

Publication History:

"Beside Me Singing in the Wilderness" *Crowded Magazine* (2014)
"Onanon" *Shadows & Tall Trees* (2014)
"Greener Pastures" *Aghast #1* (2015)
"A Discreet Music" *Aickman's Heirs* (2015)
"The Devil Under the Maison Blue" *The Dark* (2015)
"The Inconsolable" *Cemetery Dance* (2016)
"Dancers" *Strange Aeons* (2016)
"Bookends" *The Journal of Unlikely Entomology* (2014)

All other stories are published here for the first time.

Cover art and illustrations by Michael Bukowski
Digital layout by K. Allen Wood

Praise for *Greener Pastures*

"Michael Wehunt's *Greener Pastures* is a wonderful collection of quietly creepy tales that are mature and smart enough to let their effects linger. An impressive debut. Just stay away from that house where your favorite weird horror movie was filmed, okay?"

—**Paul Tremblay**, author of *A Head Full of Ghosts* and *Disappearance at Devil's Rock*

"With *Greener Pastures*, Michael Wehunt creates visions of creeping dread and transfiguration that lift a trope-heavy genre into the realm of existential poetry. There are things in here I've never seen before, some of which I devoutly hope to never see again. The stories thus collected trace a journey through the heartland of an America that's unfamiliar yet primordially recognizable, stripped down to its red-soaked roots and bones--the squirming heartstrings of a nation founded by heretics and outlaws, in all its irreligious ecstasy. Occasional spasms of regret and terror aside, you'd kick yourself for not coming along."

—**Gemma Files**, award-winning author of *Experimental Film* and the Hexslinger series

"Weird, emotionally complex, Kafkaesque, dread-filled: I might apply all these terms and more to Michael Wehunt's collection *Greener Pastures*. It's one of the finest debuts I've read in years. Wehunt understands that true strangeness comes out of the personal, and that true horror is what happens during the complex interactions between real human beings. *Greener Pastures* is outstanding work."

—**Steve Rasnic Tem**, award-winning author of *Deadfall Hotel, Blood Kin,* and *Ubo*

"Moving through landscapes rendered with a poet's precision, the characters in Michael Wehunt's compelling stories confront deep mysteries of the self and the world. In the process of plumbing the unremembered and the unknown, Wehunt's characters undergo transformations catastrophic and sublime, occasioned and spurred by their growing contact with the hidden portions of themselves and their surroundings. Wehunt skillfully invokes the history of horror fiction and film even as he is at work crafting the genre's future, in one of the more remarkable debuts in recent memory."

—**John Langan**, author of *Sefira and Other Betrayals*

"Michael Wehunt's stories are a landscape of the strange and uncanny that his characters navigate with compasses fashioned from loss, sorrow, and solitude. Often, the true horror is not what they find at the end of the journey, but what they discover within themselves along the way. Unsettling, emotionally resonant, and beautifully written, *Greener Pastures* is an impressive debut."

—**Damien Angelica Walters**, author of *Sing Me Your Scars* and *Paper Tigers*

"Occasionally the Horror genre sees authors who simply emerge out of the aethyr fully formed, their vision striking and their voice unique. Michael Wehunt is one such specimen. His fiction is a delicate wedding of Raymond Carver-style humanism and the authentically nightmarish. *Greener Pastures* is a book that stirred in me feelings of awe, terror, and envy. Wehunt is an astonishing talent."

—**Richard Gavin**, author of *Sylvan Dread*

"Michael Wehunt understands that terror and grief are necessarily conjoined—and in these stories, he draws them nearer still, employing deft skills that recall those of Peter Straub, Robert Aickman and Jorge Luis Borges. Watch out for this one: Wehunt will break your heart and chill your bones."

—**David Nickle**, author of *Eutopia: A Novel of Terrible Optimism*

"A deft and subtle collection of terrors, full of precise observations and chiseled language, and shot through with genuine dread. Michael Wehunt's *Greener Pastures* strikes me as how it must feel to be watching a sunset and suddenly realize you're being bitten all over by something you can't see, softly at first, and then harder and harder as whatever it is realizes you can't move. These tales have a remarkable, almost pastoral sense of calm at moments, which lulls the reader and makes their disturbances all the more palpable."

—**Brian Evenson**, author of *A Collapse of Horses* and *Last Days*

"The stories in Michael Wehunt's collection, *Greener Pastures*, move from quietly tender to coldly vicious effortlessly, like the gentle breeze of a fall before hitting the jagged rocks below. These stories are united by the author's beautiful mastery of evocative language and darkly elegant imagery. Whether bathing in blood falls, listening to ghosts reveal terrible secrets hidden in the insides of jazz, to the monstrous footprints of a beast carrying inconsolable sorrow, *Greener Pastures* is a virtuoso performance of everything there is to love in dark fiction."

—**Bracken MacLeod**, author of *Mountain Home* and *Stranded*

"As though sprung from the forehead of Zeus, Michael Wehunt has come abruptly onto the scene with the seasoned maturity of a veteran. His stories are lighted way-stations in the dark and unnavigable territory between the beautiful and the horrific. If he's this good now, I can't wait to see what he has in store for us in the future."

—**Nathan Ballingrud**, author of *North American Lake Monsters*

"Most fiction can be categorized by its preoccupation with either form or content. Devotees of both camps claim superiority. Yet the best fiction—that which moves and challenges in equal measure—pushes the limits of form while fearlessly plumbing the depths of experience and consciousness. Michael Wehunt is tackling enormous, timeless questions about human life— our impulse toward conflict, our lust for immortality, our endless need for connection and communication—and simultaneously exploring the boundaries of written expression. His experiments with structure and language will attract notice but it's the unsettling yet recognizable desires driving his characters that will resonate and linger in memory. This delightful debut collection represents the early days of what will no doubt be a remarkable career."

—**S.P. Miskowski**, author of the Skillute Cycle

For Natalia, everything.

If you have ever gone to the woods with me,
I must love you very much.

—Mary Oliver

Contents

Of Insects, Angels, and People Too Tired to Go On

by Simon Strantzas

Sometimes, it's easy to forget that nothing is really cyclical. We like to talk about what's old being new again, and consider our culture to simply be a series of rehashes of what came before. But it doesn't work that way. Life is a continuum, where everything before builds up to everything now.

It's this way with the Horror genre. We talk about it having waves, about how interest in it fades during years of prosperity and increases during periods of social upheaval. We mention that even if the vampire is replaced in the cultural zeitgeist by the zombie, it's only a matter of time before the vampire returns to reclaim its throne for another term.

All of this masks a truth that every Horror fan really ought to know by now: when things come back, they come back different.

What I'm trying to get at is this: what we call Horror changes. What came before is a foundation for what we have now, just as what's now will be a foundation for the future.

1

Horror grows. It evolves. And how it does this is by invading other genres and styles of storytelling. Horror absorbs and transforms everything into itself. We come up with different names for it—Dark Fantasy, Magical Realism, the Weird—but it's a single dark and twisted lens, one capable of revealing great insights about ourselves... assuming we can bear to open our eyes long enough to peer through it.

The current state of Horror is interesting. Granted, there are still adherents to the old tropes of the genre, who enjoy telling and reading the same sorts of stories they grew up with; but there is also a new wave of Horror that builds upon that past, while increasingly fusing with other genres toward the future. As a result, some of Horror's newest and brightest practitioners find themselves detouring from the cosmicism of Lovecraft to visit the hyper- and super-realities of Kafka, Borges, and Aickman, where fantastical elements are used more metaphorically, and with a gentler, subtler brush, to illuminate the inherent strangeness of our postmodern existence.

Which brings me, finally, to *Greener Pastures*, the debut collection from Michael Wehunt you hold in your hands. As one of those aforementioned newest and brightest practitioners, he has only been active in Horror and Weird circles for a few short years, but in that time he's managed to garner a reputation for delivering strange and bizarre stories that exist in the overlap of Horror, Fantasy, and Literary fiction. Any of these camps could reasonably claim him. The fact that he considers himself one of us—a Weird Horror writer—is evidence of the growing trend of respect Horror is receiving at the tail end of this decade, and how that respect is trickling down to new writers. It's authors like Wehunt that help show the world that Horror is more than the set of tropes that has defined it for too long, and instead is a transformative mode of writing that stretches out and affects all serious forms of literature.

My attention was first drawn to Michael Wehunt's work by C.M. Muller, editor of *Nightscript* journal, who directed me to a piece of fiction posted online. Muller was enthusiastic about this unfamiliar writer, and his enthusiasm prompted me to read the short piece. By the end, I understood precisely why Muller had been so excited. I mentioned this tale to Michael Kelly, editor of *Shadows & Tall Trees*, who reminded me that he, too, had published a piece by Wehunt in that Word Fantasy Award-nominated journal, and urged me to immediately read "Onanon." Reading that story concretized my belief that there was a serious talent in our midst.

Wehunt's work is emotional and complex. He understands both the excruciating pain and the exquisite beauty of being alive. Take "A Discreet Music." Here is a story about a man who lives at odds with his love for his wife, his commitment to her, and the torch he has carried for years for another. And while he's dealing with this, and the guilt it brings, he is also undergoing a physical transformation that threatens to at once both free and confine him. Wehunt's willingness to eschew easy answers to this tumult of emotions brings to mind the work of writers like Steve Rasnic Tem, who understand the inherent power of the personal, and how the surreal and fantastic can be used to amplify that power to greater affect the reader. This doesn't come easy to most, and it cements the importance of emotional honesty in Wehunt's work.

But when Wehunt decides to frighten, which he does a number of times in these pages, he doesn't hold back. His horrors are not of the gruesome variety, but instead resonate with terror and dread. Look no further than at the sweeping history of "Beside Me Singing in the Wilderness," a tale that spans a lifetime, starting with a strange encounter in the mountains, and ending in blood. The immediate scope of the story is contained between those two points, yet the implications of what has happened and what it means speaks to something far older and ancient. It's cosmic horror without the cosmos. Or, perhaps, "October Film Haunt: *Under the House*" will press more of your buttons. It certainly presses all of mine. I don't think I've encountered a story that brought me such unadulterated terror outside of an Adam Nevill novel. The trappings are familiar, but the pacing and reveal are communicated with intensity and deft skill, clawing their way into your psyche. It's certainly a standout story in an already standout book.

And that's the thing, isn't it? Standing out? As fringe culture's influence on the mainstream grows and dominates, many areas in its corona that were once written off or ignored are suddenly finding new popularity. It's certainly happening to Horror. The number of new writers entering the field has not been rivaled since the height of last century's Horror boom, and I can only assume it's because the idea of writing in the Horror mode is losing the stigma it once had. Younger writers are understanding that they no longer have to hide their love of the dark. They don't have to abandon it. Writing Horror is a legitimate path for the serious author at the moment, even if not yet a financially viable one. With this increased number of writers entering the field, it's getting harder for authors to get noticed. It takes serious work and dedication, and commitment to the craft. After reading *Greener Pastures*, it's clear Michael Wehunt has all this. But he also has something else: a unique vision and way to express it. That's a rare gift, and it helps elevate him from the crowd.

So pour yourself a drink, sit back, and enjoy what Mr. Wehunt has to show you here. There are stories about insects, about angels, about people too tired to go on. There are stories that will disturb you. But you won't be able to look away. These tales will get into your head and change you in ways you won't expect. That's just what Wehunt does.

Nothing you can do about it now but give in and accept the consequences.

Simon Strantzas
Toronto, Canada
November 2015

Beside Me Singing in the Wilderness

Sissa died last year, just shy of our hundred and thirtieth birthday. I ain't talked much to folks since, excepting Mr. Pearl. Me and Sissa was both childless. But I've shook it off and traveled such a long way at my brittle age. I've come home to this nameless mountain pouring blood from its bowel.

Mr. Pearl stands beside my wheelchair watching the bloodfall. It's closer to a trickle now, whether through time clotting some wound or through holes in my memory I can't be sure. I'm humming snatches of hymns Sissa and me made up in our girlhood. Mr. Pearl takes this last chance to ask my age—he's been mighty curious these last two decades—and I tell him. He gives a sly look, then whistles and says he thought I was at least forty years younger. I say thanks but that's still old as bones. He laughs, though it's a laugh with a shiver inside.

This far up in the Georgia wilderness you can near enough spit clean into North Carolina. The air smells of recent snow and pine and spruce. It still seems a quiet land,

7

1: strange setting

but when I was a child any folk in these mountains was little more than a mote in the world's eye.

I spent just shy of a month here. Sissa and me had just turned seven and shared one button-eyed doll between us. Mama moved us nearby after Daddy got crushed under a locomotive down in Atlanta. We was supposed to start afresh in the new township Mama'd heard tell of. They had plans of a lumber mill down at the mountain's foot and a town hall and even a school for us little ones. Such life that would've bustled not half a mile from where I'm sitting withered in this chair.

But it wasn't long before somebody found the bloodfall. It spewed forth in them days. A man called Jessup come tearing into the village, what had of late been christened Adepine, his mouth dripping red. Two of the elders had to put him down with buckshot. Folk set out to find what it was he'd got into and within days there was screams tearing at the trees and settlers strung dead across the mountainside, Mama among them. Winter of 1889. I don't recollect the exact date. I miss Sissa fierce, but there's times I can't hardly remember Mama. Faces from before the blood are swallowed up.

Mr. Pearl looks down at me, and I see the place eating at him. The smile on his lips is that of a starved wolf. His glasses like new pennies in the blood's glare. I can't say what it is bleeding in that rock, but I know how it pulls at you. A magnet tugging at the meat in your head. How the taste of iron gets in your throat and makes you powerful thirsty.

So I dismiss him before he can step over to the pool. I've left him the money I got from all six of my husbands, for he's done fine by me. Never was I in want of better caretaking. He carted me four hundred and some-odd miles from Charlottesville, even pushed me the last few of them. He's reluctant to leave, but with a troubled "You take care now, Miz Alma," he starts picking his way back down to the car.

A slow hush falls. The pool stains its rim of snow and the land presses around me. It is bitter cold.

I tip forward and unfold myself. The wheelchair rolls back along the flattened ground. I ain't been upright in a pile of blue moons but already I feel those decades shedding like dead skin. All the same it's a passing notion. My heart still sags with time as ever it did.

And there's other folk up here, off around the mountainside but getting closer. I can feel them in my joints. Some are bound to stumble across this pocket of the world now and again, I suppose. Even in the deep of winter, toothless as it is this far south. Lord, don't let them find this place. Though I reckon I'm wasting my breath on that one. Seems the Lord ain't listened to my voice in an age, if ever He did.

I hole up in the log shack, inside the trees a ways from the clearing. It's a ruin of a thing, much like myself, and it was here when I was but a child. After so many years, the soil must be mystified that either the shack or me still stands upon it.

I heft this plastic jug and knock its lid off. Mr. Pearl had to tote it up here because just hours ago I surely couldn't have brought it off the floor. Still I rest a while before I start drinking Sissa's life. Soon my belly's fit to bust and I need to prepare for the coming day. Sleeping's one of the few things I got in common with regular folk so it's long been precious to me. I go over to the bed. Sorry thing looks as if it's been used by every critter under the sun. One more won't hurt.

*

Time rippling out. It's like a lake that won't ever calm after a stone skips across it.

I remember us fleeing through that long midday. Pieces

9

of the settlers flung about the clearing by the pool, making red dents in the fresh snow. The drifts reached up to our knees in places, Sissa holding my hand as we ran, the both of us painted in blood. The sun was blinding upon all that white.

I remember the cave we found, a black mouth with pursed lips we had to wriggle our way into. It was set into the mountain's face a mile or more from the bloodfall. We laid up hiding, not sure if any of the townsfolk was still about and seeking us. We listened to the plink of water neverending down in the cave's throat and murmurs drifting up in the blackness before we taught ourselves how to build a fire. Something moved deep in those tunnels below, a stirring of life against rock.

I remember how Sissa sung them first nights through with her perfect and tuneful voice, a miracle to hear even in her youth. She tried singing hymns we got from Mama and church at the first, me humming her some harmony, but when we did so a burning filled us. Loathsome pain we could feel squirming in our blood. Same thing with our fumbling prayers. The cave clouding with a moist stench. The rustle of that something down in the dark. Wasn't long till we fashioned our own new words and I'd sit there in cold we couldn't feel anymore and listen to Sissa's golden tongue. They were hymns a shade or two blacker and they seemed to please the mountain into sleep.

I remember feeling I'd become a part of that mountain and ever what was curled up within it. We stayed for a long while, wondering which among God's creatures didn't eat nary a thing. It was a frightful time and soon we didn't rightly recall what hunger was, nor thirst, excepting the raw blood we were in want of. That blood we swore upon each other's names not to hunt though it wore at us.

I remember being still young things, thirteen or thereabouts, when the mountain's lips parted enough for our bigger selves to fit through. Sissa and me tried to fit back into the world, too. Awful lonesome had been our years in that forgotten hole, even being twins, and it wasn't no better once we come down from it and existed beyond the edges of towns, stealing line-hung clothes and eating what we could get our hands on. So one clear-skied morning found us standing in the town square of Callum, North Carolina, and we watched the way people lived. We'd forgot.

I remember us going to the Baptist church there the first Sunday, such hope in our breasts. How we saw one another's eyes crust black one step inside the vestibule and our skin cracking like tree bark. The blood in us hot and unrestful as we staggered outside, soiled and wretched things that we was. Churchgoers still milling in the dirt yard began to scream. We sought a new township but did not set our shameful feet on any more hallowed ground. For it was certain we carried the mountain with us.

I remember budding. Coming to know how beautiful I was, and how being provided for was a simple thing because of it. What our scents did to men. I remember the first I married, Werther, and how his callused hands felt on my skin. We wed in 1897. The trespass of his organ inside of me, inside the slick redness always there, my barren womb cleaning itself at all times like a mind in denial.

I remember the taste of every one of my husbands and I remember their graves. Marble stones etched with my hope that their lives was good to them. That somehow I was good to them. We were no hunters of the night, me and Sissa, and even when our bodies began to wither from the awful starvation, we did not go seeking nourishment. This starvation became the story we tried to tell ourselves, as we both tried to keep our faces turned to the Christian sun, to keep the shadows we held stuck in their corners. My husbands knew no ill, though they attended Sunday services alone. And dined alone, lest I wanted to puke it up after. But

I could have done far worse evils.

And I remember Sissa, always near. She never did agree to marry and so lived with me through all my matrimonies. She lived for me, I came to realize. Though I embraced the world, its pleasures and its sorrows, it was with Sissa that I was home. We'd often cling together in the nights, drawing comfort in one another. Sissa would sing and I'd listen and that was when we could shut out all this life that just wouldn't quit us.

But at the start of it I remember bathing in the bloodfall, me and Sissa together, opening our jaws to take it in. We drank deep of its salty richness. All around us were the snarls and the breaking of bone as the mountain's blood boiled in the veins of the settlers. Alone we watched clearheaded and whole. Not knowing how we was any different.

We had all the earth's time ahead of us and still we'd never come to understand. Least not in a way a woman could hope to reconcile in her endless heart.

*

In the shack I wake to a face right above mine. Wide eyes staring shock-wild. Figures kneel around my bed, shining in a wedge of moonlight held in the doorway.

They're young, three men and two women swallowed up by coats and scarves. Heavy packs strapped to their shoulders. Between hanging sheaves of blood-matted hair, the nearest girl swipes a coarse, wet tongue across my mouth. My heart would seize, if it could.

"Git," I yell into their crowding faces. Red smears around their mouths. They been drinking from the pool. "There's nothing here for you all!" I slither from the bed on all fours toward them and they scamper like vermin back into the silver dark.

They're weak and new and atremble. My blood is strong

12

here. I got nothing to fear from the likes of them, so I drift back into clouds and sleep a while.

❀

Sissa took her blood out. Said she couldn't stand it another day. "I desire true sleep, Alma," she told me not long before. "This ain't natural. I'm so tired."

"We both are tired, Sissa." And I laid my hand on her cheek.

When she was gone, I realized I'd forgot to ask her to sing for me one last time. That voice from on high. Sissa sounded like an angel, even if she was never allowed to be one.

So I've brought her tainted blood back to where we got it when we was just little girls. It sits heavy in my gut. I reckon I brought mine back too, for I can hear it swishing through me in its old circles.

❀

Down through the dawn new snow's falling and new blood's spilling on it, for those folks who broke my sleep with their peculiar vigil are tearing themselves apart by the pool. Three of them are still in one piece, hissing blood-crazed a stone's throw from my door. A woman pulls out the eye of the only man left, and for an instant—the sun peeking over the crowns of the mountains like a curious child—he looks right at me with his mess of a face. Then she's at his throat, and he falls with legs kicking.

I seen this all before. It is wearisome. Mamas pulling the guts out of their own babies, just for the doing. I seen my own Mama come at Sissa with her teeth bared and I can still feel the weight of the chunk of rock I used to fend her off.

I walk over to the pool and get down on my knees beside

it. Could be the Lord hollowed this mountain out with His own hands, though what foul thing He laid in that womb only He might know. For I surely can't believe it's the blood of Christ issuing forth. Could be the Lord is blind to it, and some god beyond my tongue was wounded something grievous in the depths of the mountain and history.

That wound's slowed some and I dearly hope it scabs over. Or folks'll keep on drinking its blood and getting like rabid dogs from it. I reckon I can't know why not Sissa and me. Because of us being twins, or because of the blood having some deeper purpose for us and for this baptism far from the folds of salvation.

Soon one ragged girl remains. She stumbles off. Maybe down into the world, likely just to a gibbering death somewhere among the pines, dirtying this vast white blanket. Better for her to freeze.

Quiet fills the cracks in the air back up. I jam a finger down my throat. Sissa's blood that I drunk from the jug comes splashing up, hot with acid, and mixes with that of the mountain.

I pull out Mr. Pearl's straight razor to flash in the light. It's cold and has a handle to match his name.

I wish Sissa had held on a little while longer. Or maybe I just wish I hadn't held on after her. It would be fine to have her here, as I open my veins to give all this back to whatever gave it. The blood curls and twitches coming out. The mountain leans over me. I can feel it wanting me to keep its gift, to grow as old as its bones, but I will not witness what it's planned for me. I will not become its child or its emissary.

Yes, it would be fine to have Sissa here beside me, singing our old hymns in our own words. To watch the white world grow finally dark, fading to the same red as our tiresome lives and all this stained snow.

Onanon

He'd missed Christmas and her last two birthdays, but his mother looked the same, a husk that never seemed to age. They sat at a short oval table, her walker standing sentry on its hollow aluminum legs. When he could take the silence no longer, the tick of the antique clock beside her stove, Adam laid four white pages beside her. A nurse passed by the open door, humming something he almost recognized. He repeated "Mom" in a soft cadence until her face lifted and found him.

"I remember Dad telling me once," he said, "not long before his heart attack, that you were born in Norway. He said Amanda wasn't your birth name, but for some reason you never told him what it was."

She focused in on him. He had a hard time looking at her in these rare moments because she never blinked. Her eyes would dry out as she stared.

"Is that right, Mom?" He reached over and picked up the cold bones of her hand and held them. "What was your name?"

She was still. Her pupils dilated and the hazel darkened. Her thin grayed hair reached past the rails of her collarbones.

15

He tried to remember the woman she once was, but a distance had been in place from his earliest memories. She'd spent far more time staring out her bedroom window than with her only child. He was still a boy the last time he'd gotten anything more than her sad parting sentiment. But now her mouth opened wide as though tasting the air and she said, "Some say it is Dronning." He was amazed as ever at the crisp enunciation in her voice, despite the loss of all her teeth more than twenty years earlier.

"Dronning." Adam watched their twined hands and took a shaky breath. "I think you were mentioned in a story a girl I know wrote. Does the name Meli Gramia ring a bell?"

He thought she almost smiled then but she would say nothing else. Her face was directed back into her other world now. Every visit he asked her pointlessly where she'd gone when he was a boy, but today he didn't. Instead he waited in her silence a while longer before hugging her goodbye.

"You will be my son," he heard as he turned to close the door behind him. But she always said that.

•

You lay in the dark and heard the wet parting of my mouth. Warmth dripped onto your face from above the bed, where I clung in a corner of the room.

You closed your eyes against the scuttle of fingernails across the ceiling. When I was gone the room hung in quiet. You threw the sheets away from yourself and went to the window and twisted the blinds open. Below, figures on all fours skulked behind parked cars. Another watched you among the low bones of dogwood trees. The line of them stretching to the right, their petals gone.

In the fog of your breath you wrote MOTHER on the glass.

GREENER PASTURES

You wrote DRONNING, and I had never filled your heart more.

*

He'd never thought Meli was the girl's name, even when she murmured it against his neck the night they'd met at a reading in September. She was the earthy type he'd pick out of a room first, twenty-ish, hovering at the fringe of the bookstore. Milk skin with grease spot freckles, high rounded cheekbones and dense black hair. A girl who wore scarves in late summer, more like a Jennifer or a Karen, something that buried the truth of her under a soft screen.

Afterward she'd quoted one of Adam's old stories and complimented the rhythm of his sentences. They both agreed he was better than the guy they'd listened to. Her praise and the way her body moved and he was half in love. In bed she asked a lot of questions about his childhood and he gave answers that even he thought were foggy. She was insatiable and let him do everything but stick his tongue in her mouth.

He'd woken alone in the early morning and found the sheets speckled with flowers of her blood.

Though Meli had softly demurred when he asked about her own work, she left a manuscript beside his laptop. A surreal story about a woman who believes she has become a great queen and explains her new status to her son. It was titled "Amanda," the same as his mother and his stalled novel. From the first sentence the hours fell away and a vague despair built up around him.

Her prose read like it burned in her blood and spattered out of her. But she also wrote as if she had the time to pick up every seashell on some prehistoric beach, examine the sound inside each one until she found that inimitable tone.

He spent the day curled up staring at those twenty-nine pages, flipping back and forth to find so many passages beating with raw life. He felt sick with envy of a gift that was lifetimes beyond his own.

A few nights ago they'd run into each other—or she'd found him—at a release party for a poetry chapbook. Incestuous little circles of writers. They steeped themselves in drink and weed. Same as before, she wouldn't talk about her work, and sometime in the night she left him. He woke tangled in sheets sprinkled with more bloodstains and heavy with her scent. A new manuscript lay on the floor beside the bed. It was titled "Dronning," with the byline "from a novel by Adam Storen."

His head throbbed at the seams. He wadded the bedding up into the trash chute. Dripped whiskey in his coffee and crawled back onto the stripped mattress with the story.

It was more scene than plot, twelve hundred words that cut off with a face in the window of a mountain cabin. The strange and singing prose was still there but had diminished over some dark threshold. The words felt ill, somehow, concerned as they were with some implied creature on the periphery of the page.

Yet something in the writing opened its jaws and he could almost hear them creak as he placed his head inside.

*

When he got back from questioning his mother, he booted his laptop and opened the bloated file of his novel. It sagged there half-written in its window, the cursor blinking at him. *Amanda.* She was so murky to him that he couldn't even fictionalize her. His own words rode together as neat and hemmed as cars in traffic. Tuneless things. Dry as his mother's eyes. He'd been plugging square blocks into the round holes in his childhood.

GREENER PASTURES

Eleven months out of work for the Great American Novel. He'd cashed in the paltry 401k and it would be fumes by spring. Edging into his thirties and this was what he'd slopped his soul into. He skimmed the first chapter but couldn't make it through. He started drinking instead.

Meli's stories sat on the desk. He lifted them and let the pages flutter. He sat and wished he could have her again, bed sheets be damned. Stronger still was a sort of hatred for her and the resonance of her words. He opened the trash bin icon at the bottom of the screen. Dragged the novel into it and clicked EMPTY and a thousand hours were gone.

*

The nights grew into things rimmed with glare, like days with their bulbs just clicked off and afterimages burned into his eyes. He drank. He stood at his fourth floor window and watched the parked cars below. Thought he saw a face peering from the black beneath his old VW Rabbit. The bare dogwoods shivered along the street, and a sense of standing within the girl's story draped over him. He heard a sound outside his door and pressed an ear to the wood, his glass clinking ice in a hand he couldn't still.

In the sleepless dark he stared at the ceiling above his bed. The threads of a memory brushed him, a boy looking up and waiting for a shape to fill the corner, until the room turned from black to gray.

*

According to Google, *dronning* was Norwegian for "queen." The word, the thought of it, gave him a vague panic.

He spent hours searching for Meli Gramia online. He trawled bars and readings. Chased her like a legend but she seemed less than a ghost. In the end he thought to use the words in "Dronning" to find her. Certain descriptions were a little too detailed, as though she'd spelled things out for him. Drawn him a map in prose.

So he left the city for the rust of nature. It struck him as a thing many lost and grasping writers did. He brought a fresh journal in the event she was leading him on a wild goose chase. He'd find a place to stay and take a break instead. Now that the novel was gone he meant to recapture the art of the short, which had made what faint name he'd enjoyed back in the days when people whispered about his potential.

Following the route in Meli's story trimmed a good chunk off the drive and soon he passed through the creases between mountains. The Rabbit wasn't happy as the land rose up but it made the trip without shuddering apart. He parked in the V of two low hills. The cabin was situated there in the way she'd written, "curled in the elbow of a dead giant." Beyond it the Appalachians began their long course north. He stood in the dooryard and the shallow air, holding the better part of his recent life in a cardboard box. The place was a comforting trope with its uneven, knotted planks and thin chimney jutting from the end of the roof like a straw in a cup. It was half porch. It was perfect.

He stepped through the unlocked door and breathed the dust. Put the box down on the scarred table next to the wood stove. An ancient beehive the length of his forearm hung from the ceiling. Someone had tied a yellow ribbon just above the top of it. On the narrow bed was a sheaf of papers with "Onanon" crouching in the center of the top page. Beneath it in a leaning scrawl were the words "read & remember." He didn't move for some time. He stared at the pages and listened to a sort of quiet he'd never heard. Through the three windows dusk dropped quick and finally he went to the box and opened one of the bottles of whiskey he'd let himself bring.

In "Dronning" the writer had texted the girl. He found

the story in the box and skimmed it. The number was right there on page three. Phone reception was spotty but outside he had one bar and a wavering second. Halfway through the bottle he left a voicemail letting her know he'd made it to the cabin and was about to crack open her latest opus in the lonesome bunched wilderness. He told her if that didn't get her up here he'd eat her words.

He sat at the edge of the porch in a splintered rocking chair. The sky spread and wide stars punched through to glimmer down at him. Trees gathered in the dark. Already the cold was deep, the first of November crawling down the mountainsides. He got up and slipped a hooded sweatshirt over his head and sat back down. His phone lay mute against his thigh.

*

My love, I hunched on the roof. The whisper of my hands rasping above on the shingles. Splinters in my palms. Beyond the streaks of the windows mountains sharpened toward you in the starred black. The world leaned in to see.

I had to leave you those years ago. I sought my home. My husbands and at last my sleep. But I woke old as earth with you in my nostrils. I woke in a new and ready season. You spoke my name and I had never filled your heart more.

"Dronning," you said, and the sound was ripe, your chin wet with drool and blood. You listened to the vacuum as I took the split moon into my mouth and the stars tipped in behind it and the sun struggled up above the peaks. You slept and the windows filled and opened.

You will be my son. Remember the nights in your child-bed.

*

Late morning he set off into the wild blur of color. Spruces and pines and oaks. He thought of the girl not calling back. The journal was in one back pocket, her latest pages folded into the other. He searched for a first sentence of his own but kept circling back to the opening words of "Onanon." *I put my tongue inside you, Adam.* He bent over waiting to vomit. The sun beat almost summer-hot through the foliage. He sat down in the dead leaves and tried to read the first paragraph over and over. The words swam away and sank into his stomach where they soured. It was hours before he looked up and saw the humps of the mountains were cutting the light.

His phone buzzed on the table when he came back. A text from Meli, "did u read it." He smiled though he didn't want to and thumbed out "I'm trying. Where are you?"

The whiskey bottle cast sweetened light onto the table. He watched it shifting then went out on the porch instead. Opened the journal and licked the tip of his pencil like some old grizzled novelist and stared at the lined page.

An hour and he'd written, *Honeybees coated the hill.* He tapped the words with the pencil. He stood up and went inside and came back out with four fingers of whiskey in a plastic cup. Dark swallowed the cabin. He sat on the warped boards of the porch and listened to the crackle of movement in the trees.

*

After fitful sleep Adam woke to another "did u read it" on the screen of the phone. His head felt like shards rubbing against one another. He got up and noticed a photograph pinned to the floor under the night table. A shot of the cabin, framed so that the trees all reached toward it, giving the scene almost the effect of a fisheye lens. The image was washed out with a smudge of black on the roof. He rubbed at it with his thumb but it was part of the picture.

He tossed it onto the bed and found some aspirin in the cardboard box. Eggs wouldn't stay down but he wished he had them anyway. He chewed on a granola bar and texted Meli back. Circled the cabin and sat on the porch with the journal open on his lap. Noon came and the mountains felt redder than yesterday. He hadn't added a thing to the four lousy words about the bees.

He snapped the pencil in two. Left the journal behind and took "Onanon" into the woods. Against the scabbed trunk of a pine he nodded off then lurched awake to the sound of someone wading through dead leaves deeper in the trees. He heard someone laugh in a high voice. A bird strangled a cry in the distance and quiet rippled out from it.

I coupled behind stars, the first page began. At least he thought that was what he read. Earlier it had been something different but he couldn't be sure. "Dronning" was simple enough; it was strange but it was made of words. This new one made his eyes ache. Like reading worms instead. The things on the page wouldn't stay still.

On the second page he managed to read a paragraph about the mother burying her teeth in the dirt beneath a cabin before returning to her family. To ready her son and herself. Looping migraine phrases. He found himself weeping and the sun halved the sky and the letters on the page changed. *A hive swarmed and you opened your mouth. When you were a boy I folded myself into your bed and suckled you. Sowing your blood and murmuring songs of home. The time to leave was nearing. Mountains mossed red yellow gold called from their roots over the horizons. I paused, humming, and fed my saliva between your lips.*

He lay down in the leaves and watched the cloudless sky through the trees.

•

23

A second photo, creased with time, waited on the night table. A young Adam sleeping, posters on the wall of his first bedroom, the blood leached from his face in the slight overexposure. He had to squint to be certain but there was an insect spreading its wings beneath one eye and another bridging his lips. The vantage point looked down from a high angle above the head of the bed. His arms were tucked at his sides under the blanket and a shadow draped across his chest, trailing out from something tubelike just reaching into the left side of the frame.

He crumpled the photo and let it fall. A few minutes of furtive searching turned up nothing creepy or crawly in the eaves or along the edges of the walls. The old hive hung full of dust above the stove.

Two days up here and he was moving in circles. He took a fresh bottle of Bushmill's out into the falling cold and saw three more photographs taped to the porch posts.

In the first he was a boy again, even younger than the picture back in the cabin, cradled in his bed by a mass of black. He saw vague arms holding him, a dark blur reaching toward his mouth, but whatever it was hadn't translated through the lens.

He tore the second photo down and saw his father lying tangled in sheets and the limbs of a woman. A film of sudden sweat made him shiver. It was Meli. She should have been a child when his dad was alive, but right there was the same too-pretty face, the same spill of black hair, the same blood spotted on the sheets. Her arm lifted toward Adam, holding the camera in a lovers' self-portrait.

He peered at the last photo, his nose almost smudging it. After a moment what he was seeing clicked. Bees covered a figure seated in a wooden chair. There was enough in the frame to recognize his mother's room in the nursing home. The figure's face, openmouthed and entirely coated in the bees, was turned to a closed window.

Beyond the porch the trees gave up nothing as he scanned them, listening for the rustle of footsteps. Silence clustered and he thought of shouting Meli's name into it.

Instead he sat and wrote about his mother and father. This time he didn't embellish. He wrote of a boyhood that had always felt like a gray smear. No family portraits, the three of them smiling off toward the photographer's hand. No beach trips. Just school years and few friends and always being tired. He remembered a telescope he still felt guilty about seldom using. He chewed on a new pencil but couldn't dredge up anything so disturbing from before the day his mother climbed out her bedroom window and disappeared.

She was gone for seventeen months. He'd watched his father give up hope, not quite understanding the hope himself. His parents had done little more than live in the same house. He was thirteen when she returned one night, her clothes stained and hanging off her as she stood swaying beside his bed. She'd lost all her teeth. Two days later she was taken to the home.

A half hour drained along with the late afternoon light as he sat and tried to remember why she'd been sent away. For her own good, Dad had said. So she could feel better.

Memory became hazier still then. He remembered a woman, or women, haunting his home at night, faces reluctant to swim to his recall. Now Meli's face plugged itself in. His father had receded from him, grayed and shriveled until the week after Adam graduated high school, when he succumbed to heart failure in his sleep. Adam had spent a few more months in the house before selling it and moving to the city. He'd started writing. After only a few years his stories began to appear in journals, culminating with *Harper's* in '05 and *The New Yorker* the following year. Inevitably, he published a collection that many admired but nobody read.

He scratched this all in the journal. Even the rehashing

of his lost glories eased him. But nothing both specific and profane in his memory bobbed to the surface.

He hugged himself and wished he'd brought a jacket against the chill. Meli's words were making him sick. That had to be it. They were in his sinuses and tingling in his fingers like pine needles. He went inside and found a lighter in the cardboard box. He pulled "Onanon" from his pocket and sat on the porch steps. The million trees whispered around him now.

He scraped the wheel of the lighter and held it to a corner of the pages. The words or worms twitched on the paper. *Sleep in the dirt under the floor. Dream and remember. Hear the sound of your mother loping over roads and creeks and up into the mountains. From my dry and waiting mouth the proboscis emerges.*

The fire ate it all and in the last corner he read, *Stars swell in their bed. You reach over the mountains for them as a child for Mother's jewels. A moth or a magpie. I am come and you will be my son.*

Heat reached his fingers and he dropped the pages. Charring bits swirled into the yard and winked out. The skin on his fingertips blistered. He put his head in his hands and bit his tongue. Dark fell at last and he burned "Amanda" and "Dronning." He pulled the battery from his phone and lay in the bed and stared up into the corner.

*

Honeybees coated ~~the hill the tired leaves~~ *the new earth*

*

A heavy thump out on the porch woke him and he looked at the windows. Each seemed as though a face had just pulled away. He went outside into the muddled stillness and walked around the cabin twice. The stars were sprayed everywhere. The place had no foundation and he dug his way beneath it in a moment. There was a crawlspace of sorts and he wriggled inside and lay down. Black as absence. He felt something curl up beside him and he slept in its warmth, grateful.

*

A finger jabbed him in the ribs. The girl lay pressed against him, her face an inch from his. She licked his mouth with something too stiff to be a tongue.

He tried to scoot away and knocked his head against the underside of the cabin floor. Sunlight pried in nearly all the way around. He watched as Meli pawed at the dirt and plucked things out of it. "Hey," she said, her face streaked with filth, "open your hand."

"What do you want?"

"Just do it, open your hand."

He held his palm out and she poured a stream of small objects onto it. Human teeth. He wasn't about to count them but he thought there could be thirty or more. A full set.

"What the hell are these?" he said. "Why did you want me up here?" He tried to look away but couldn't. His mouth watered at the smell of her.

Meli smiled and he saw she had no teeth of her own. "You don't get it, do you?" she said, and laughed. Her speech was as strong and clear as his mother's. "What do you think you've been reading? Come on, you're a writer, we reached out to you in your own language. And in case you're a visual learner, I hoped those pictures I took would help you along a little quicker. I had to come up here just because you're so slow."

"Are these yours?" He shook the teeth in his hand.

"Look, I know you had trouble with the stories." She paused and inched toward him. Pushed her hand into his crotch. "Her style is a bit abstract, I guess. You do get that they were from Amanda, right? Dronning? Your mother is ready to make you in her image. Those are her teeth, remember? This is where she lived when she was a girl fresh across the ocean. She buried them here later. When she stopped needing them."

"You don't know me. That's what I remember." It was difficult not to push her down and climb onto her.

"Haven't you ever wondered about your mom? I would've thought up a hundred stories in all these years. Did you know she got out of the home last night? They're looking for her right now. If you put your battery back in you can listen to the voicemail."

"My mom's practically catatonic. She gave up on herself a long time ago and now she can hardly walk or string together a sentence." He reached to slap away her hand but she started kneading him through his jeans.

"Call it sleeping, what she's been doing all this time. It's what the Queen does until the petals open. Where'd she go when you were a kid? It's in the stories, dummy. Home to the old country, where she found her true husbands, her drones, and they fucked in fjords and fields beneath mountains different from these. She'd yearned for so long. Maybe that's when she gave up on life and took on something else."

Yearned, yes. Her fingers squeezed and everything he thought to say turned to vapor. A door slammed shut and the floor overhead gave a long stuttering creak.

"And maybe she came back with me in tow, her sprouting little girl. We purebreds have a quick gestation. A couple of years and I was menstruating. So I was able to watch you grow up. You don't remember me keeping your dad company while Mother had gone inside herself to wait. The nights I slept over or the night I had a little too much to

28

drink and his heart stopped beating for me."

She slipped his belt open and unzipped him. He was moaning already, trying to tell her to stop it, wanting to claw his way out from under the cabin, get to the car and drive anywhere that was away. "Maybe now is our time," she said. "Onanon, without an end, and I mean you, too," and she took him into her burning mouth and he lay in the fading light and shuddered.

She climbed from under the cabin and left him still spurting into the dirt. He barely had the strength to tug his pants back up. When he emerged, the yard was empty and the sun had fallen behind the mountains. A bulging moon lifted. The teeth were still clenched in his hand. Biting his palm. He dropped them into a pocket and fastened his belt.

He took a step toward the cabin and stopped. His mother peered out at him from a grimy window. The pane lifted up and a long pale tube slipped beneath it where her mouth should have been. It tapered and petaled. The rest of her face followed, eyes opening wide into wet holes.

"Mom?" A liquid hum came from her as she wormed through the window. It took on a melody. He recalled the nurse outside her door and something stirred further back in his mind. "Mom?"

She folded down onto all fours and scrabbled across the porch. Adam ran to his car. He was behind the wheel when he realized the keys were in the cabin. His mother dropped onto the hood and placed her hands against the windshield. Long blackened fingers splayed on the glass.

He fell from the car and fled into the trees. The hum grew. Something vast pulled at the air. His mother, he thought, singing the sky dark. Songs of home. He ran through limbs and the rising sound of birds screaming as they escaped with him.

Before long the land steepened and he came to the crook of the two hills, the cabin behind him and the far slope dipping down to the feet of the looming mountains. He saw bees dotting the ground at his feet. They had no wings. The sky was a blind expanse stretching from end to end of the earth. He gazed up at it and the stars were gone, whitish blurs in their place. As if they had been rubbed with pencil erasers.

Leaves crunched behind him as he watched the heavens flicker to violet, to orange, to the brown of rich soil. The moon broke open like a fruit and the sun was already coloring the jagged horizon again. Hands slipped around his waist and up under his shirt, barbed fingers tracing patterns on the skin of his belly. He struggled and the arms locked him in place.

Meli stepped up beside him. "Think of it as pollination," she said, "instead of trying to wrap your head around the old human evolution bit. Every hive starts with one Queen. There will be many of us. You'll get the hang of it when you feed. Look around you, the world is in bloom." He watched her tongue slip from her mouth but it kept coming, a hollow, curved thing hanging past her chin and sucking at the air. Her eyes went black and he looked away, down to the ground covered with red and yellow and gold leaves and the sluggish bees trundling over and between them.

He felt his mother's proboscis push into the base of his neck. Her humming song vibrated there and a sweet numbness spread. She caressed him and at last he was able to remember the nights she tucked him into her arms against her breast, until he fell into his childish dreams and God knew what she had done then.

"Mom," he said, his tongue hardening against the roof of his mouth.

Now she was drinking him. Three of his teeth loosened and fell from the gums. He swallowed them. A groan slipped out and his mother turned him around to her and passed his fluids back into his mouth blended with her own. He again tilted his head to the sky. He looked everywhere for its stars but saw only a great paling lens. A jar lowering, a world going on and on.

Greener Pastures

Y ou ever can't sleep?" the trucker said.

Forsyth glanced up out of his thoughts. The man standing at his table was big and worn out, his eyes raw and heavy even in the shadow of his cap's bill. He had a young face with an old beard matted on the left side, as though he'd been trying to nap against the window of his cab.

The trucker slid into the booth but Forsyth didn't answer his question at first. He felt the contradiction of road life, that of the lonesome loner. It could be nice to have company when he stopped off someplace, but he'd never been much for talk. He glanced around the diner. A couple more long-haulers sat on high stools at the counter, knives and forks chattering against their plates. The waitress was somewhere back in the kitchen. Even for a graveyard shift the place had a tired air.

Forsyth was bleary-eyed himself. Two grinding days, Little Rock to Birmingham to Atlanta and now he was racing the sun to Valdosta. Coming up on three hours of dark left, and by first light he meant to be on the cot in the back of his empty trailer. He'd have enough time for a quick snooze, and then all the state troopers in hell couldn't keep him from his daughter's sixth birthday the next night. Last week the two of them had started reading their first bedtime story together. Lizzie had fallen asleep just as the wolf huffed and puffed at the second pig's house. Forsyth couldn't wait to finish it. He'd been getting along with his ex-wife, too. No way was he losing that momentum.

The big trucker watched him across the booth. "You ever can't sleep?" he asked again.

"I got a feeling," Forsyth told him, "you're not talking about putting off a nap until you get to where you're going."

"No, I'm not." The trucker stared out the window as he spoke.

Forsyth followed his eyes. Only things out there were four rigs lined up in the gloom beyond the sodium lamps and an old Ford wagon off to the far side. Those lamps weren't doing much against the miles of night surrounding the place. Even the lights set into the diner's flat roof didn't seem to touch the lot. Still, it was just another diner along I-75. It didn't have a town around it, that was all.

Forsyth turned back to his temporary buddy. "Insomnia, then? That it?"

"Something like it," the trucker said, and his face reflected in the window seemed...Forsyth didn't want to call it spooked. Distracted, maybe. Enough years spent boxed in on tiresome roads and it was a simple thing to think a man was haunted.

"Hell, I think I've slept about every way a man can," Forsyth said. "I got used to it. How long you been hauling?"

"Three years, nearing on four."

"I get my two-year badge next month. How long you had insomnia?"

He turned and regarded Forsyth with those weary eyes. "I didn't say it was insomnia. I said it was something like it, didn't I?" And his gaze went back out the window.

"That you did, fella." Forsyth wasn't about to whet that edge in the man's voice, but he was curious. "I'm Forsyth, by the way. And before you ask, yes, that's my first name. My mother's maiden name."

He stuck his hand out but the trucker kept on searching the dark, absently turning his coffee mug around on the table. It produced a slow, maddening scrape.

"So what is it, then, if it's not insomnia?" He returned to his hash browns and eggs, left the man to his view.

"You ever wonder if anything's out there with us? When we're driving through the night and all these big gaps of world between towns? You got pieces of map where you can lay a quarter down and there's nothing under it."

"You mean the rural areas?" Forsyth asked.

He waved that aside. "No, no. That's not what I'm saying, man. I don't mean like farms and woods, this road connecting to that road so you can go from there to here. I'm talking about the *space* in between."

"I'm not sure I—"

He cut Forsyth off, really throwing himself into gear now. "I'm curious what it is that makes all that space up. And can it take notice of you. Might be the wondering that draws it. I knew a guy once, this was up in South Dakota, he'd haul loads for miles with just the headlights for company. Black as a pit out there, I can tell you. Not many lights strung along some of those roads. Well, Hitch—we called him that because he'd get bored and pick up hitchhikers—he went missing last year. Cops found his rig idling on a shoulder in the middle of nowhere. Right in one of those pieces of map."

Forsyth pushed his cold eggs away. The trucker stared at his hands for a minute before looking back outside.

"There's something about the lonely places. Something about us folks who go to them. Like rest stops. A month ago I saw Hitch at one in Virginia. Guy was peeking out of the trees behind the bathrooms whispering my name. I could hear him grinning. He started talking about the sky dripping on him, the night folded over like a blanket. He asked me to—oh Jesus."

"What?" Forsyth peered through the glass to see what had put that sudden watery groan in the trucker's last words. It was still just a parking lot, silent and waiting for cars. This place was from a faded era. He doubted it saw many customers even in the best of times. That was half the reason he'd stopped here.

"It's darker," the trucker said. "Look close and you can see everything slinking around."

Forsyth thought he was right about the dark, at least. The streetlights near the entrance, long necks on fifteen-foot stems, were out. The diner huddled in its own small glow now. An island. He could just pick out his rig—a glimpse of red paint—alongside the others, and he could see the edges of the forest that wanted to swallow it all. But nothing moved.

Forsyth tried a different tack. "All due respect, mister, I think you need to try for some of that sleep you can't seem to find. I doubt coffee's helping much." Over by the counter the two other men stood and stretched their backs. They settled caps on gray heads and made their way into the night. Forsyth caught furtive glances from both of them. A stream of cool air slipped inside. It had gotten colder as well as darker.

They sat in silence and watched the pair of old truckers pass in front of the building and dissolve into the encroaching shadows. Neither said as much but they were waiting for their rigs to chug into life, for the big headlights to cut the gravel dust.

Quiet rippled. Forsyth thought that maybe another light had fizzled out. The far end of the diner felt like another county.

The trucker looked at him. "I think those gaps between places are filling up. Something's looking for us. Couple of weeks back my mama started talking to me on the CB." He kept swiveling his coffee cup, only now Forsyth was almost glad for the sound. "I know what you're thinking, and it ain't ghosts. My mama's alive and well. Lives in Charlotte and volunteers at the hospital." His eyes dropped to the table again and he drained the mug. Set it down and went back to turning it.

"Your mama got a radio?" Forsyth would have liked some coffee himself but the waitress had yet to come back up front.

"Nah, she'd hardly know what to do with one. But I hear her. Different channels too. She tells me to pull over sometimes, get out of the cab and walk into a field and look up at the stars. Just lie down there in a bed of grass. She talks about greener pastures waiting. Get out and walk into the night, Sally—that's what she calls me, Sally. Always seems to be when it's darkest, right in the crease between midnight and that first streak of morning."

Forsyth put his head in his hands. His expected thought—something along the line of getting away from this man and back on the road—wouldn't come to him. Somehow he found himself fixated on all the blank space in the world. He felt he'd known it for some time, from the corners of his eyes. There was an awful lot of it between here and Valdosta, even on the interstate. He kept his CB off as a rule, but would he flip it on tonight when he settled into the driver's seat?

He glanced outside again and saw another light in the eave had gone dark. Their corner of the lot was the only beacon left. The light inside the diner might as well have been held in a box. It stopped inches beyond the windows.

"Some nights I see people running up a ditch to the road as I drive by," Sally said, "or standing in the trees. I'd call them pale. I'd call them pale enough to glow, except they're not. They're as dark as the dark, but I see them just fine. And then the radio starts crackling and my mama's talking me out of the truck."

"Come on now," Forsyth said, "you got to know that's not your mama. What you're talking about sounds like sirens luring sailors to their deaths or something. I mean, CB isn't what it used to be, but people still play with it."

"Whoever it is, she knows I ran away when I was eight because she and Dad put my dog down. She knows the name of the magazine she found under my mattress a few years later. Dad, now, he died ten years ago. Cancer. Never been his voice coming out of the CB."

"How come I haven't heard of this? I'm on the road about as much as you." Forsyth wanted to laugh, but instead his mind got snagged on the rest area whose lot he'd napped in earlier that morning. Anonymous brick squatting in the drone of highway traffic and Georgia pines scenting the air. All those unnoticed trees. Over the years he'd relieved himself in hundreds of those facilities. He'd bought undrinkable coffee, washed the sleep out of his eyes, even jerked off once or twice to clear his head. Lonely places, yes, Sally was right. He felt the deeper possibility of it unfurl in his head like a fever.

But no matter how empty a diner found itself, it wasn't a rest stop. It had a pulse. A constant heartbeat. He craned his neck to look for the absent waitress again.

"Well, now you have. I didn't know until Hitch told me." Sally's grin was both sly and shameful. His lips stayed pressed together inside the snarl of beard. It was the first time his face had come alive with something other than a jittery fear.

"Those two guys haven't started up their rigs yet," Forsyth said. He'd meant to just change the subject, clear that leering smile from Sally's face, but realized he was speaking one notch above a whisper. Both of them watched the black humps of the trucks still as felled trees in all that shadow. "Probably napping. Or napping with each other."

Neither man cracked a smile.

"Tonight Mama said I should stop here and rest a while. Lay my troubles on a kindred spirit, is how she put it. I don't think they like the voices of the dead. On account of the dead are the ones we've let go of." Sally pushed his cup away and stood up. "This place does seem like one of those gaps. It's not like there's much of anything out here. But you wait until you leave. You'll get it now." He looked through the window again. "I gotta take a leak."

He shuffled toward the little hallway in back. Forsyth watched him push into the men's room. He got up himself and walked over to the coffee station, grabbed a mug and filled it. Found some half and half and a spoon. When he got back to the table he saw at once that the outside light above his booth's window was the only one still lit up. The dark gathered close, pressing against the glass, and he tried not to look for things shifting in it.

He poured the creamer in and stirred his coffee. The clink of the spoon unnerved him. It was too much like an alarm bell. He needed to be on the road now in order to have any chance of getting back to Little Rock by suppertime tomorrow. But he sat there, eyes dragging to the window then yanking away. He pictured the radio in his rig and could almost hear a sea of static, and what would he do if his own mother began calling out to him from her nursing home in Tucson, edging him toward the rocks?

The dark outside was too active and all four trucks sat buried under it. No reason they should have been silent. Those two veteran truckers would idle their engines on a cold night. He'd never met one who wouldn't. Diesel ran long.

In the window he could see the restaurant's reflection, so he watched both the lot and the hallway behind him while he waited for Sally to return. He thought of the stack of books he'd bought for Lizzie's birthday. Rachel would give him a real smile for those. Their daughter was going to hit kindergarten running. And when he wheeled in the purple bicycle at the end, right around the time Lizzie thought the presents were done for the year...well, he figured Rachel might have something more than a smile to offer.

Forsyth sat there and Sally didn't come back. He kept his eye on that last bulb shining out in the dark. A white face might have drifted into sight before retreating. He wasn't sure. The key to his rig was heavy in his pocket.

In the other pocket his phone buzzed. He jumped in his seat before fishing it out. Nothing on the screen, not even "incoming call." He tapped the phone and held it up to his ear and listened.

"Daddy?" Lizzie's voice came as though she were sitting in his lap. "Daddy!"

"Baby?" His mouth went dry. "What are you doing up? You need to be in bed, hon." He said the normal things, the daddy things, his fingers pinching the bridge of his nose hard enough to hurt.

"I'm not sleepy. Come outside, Daddy. I'm in the trees."

"No, baby, you're not in the trees. You're dreaming." He started touching everything on the table, coffee cup, plate, silverware. He gripped the napkin dispenser in his hand and tried to squeeze it into something else. An anchor, anything to keep him fastened to his seat. He shouted Sally's name into the empty diner.

"He's with his mommy. Come outside, Daddy. It's my birthday. It's tomorrow now."

Forsyth nearly fell to the floor as he lurched out of the booth. He staggered across the room and down the short hall and banged into the restroom. Empty, it could have always been empty but for the window half-open in the wall above the urinal. Cold air, somehow darkened air, fell through it. The tube lights in the ceiling fizzed. He slammed the window shut and checked the single stall. A strip of tissue was draped over the toilet.

"Told you, Daddy. Come look at the stars with me. They're birthday stars."

He clamped the phone to his ear as he went back to the counter, stood by the register a moment, then pushed through the swinging door into the kitchen. "Hello?" he called. The waitress had to be here. A cook, somebody. But there was only a low murmur of talk radio voices from the back. They faded into a wash of fuzz and then his older brother whispered his name. Paul, who lived way up in Vancouver. They'd talked on the phone just last week. Forsyth heard his name again, louder, and fled back into the dining area.

"You're not my Lizzie," he said into the phone.

"Please, Daddy." His daughter's one-more-story voice, the one he'd been longing to hear, perfect down to the pleading end. "Come finish. I want to know if the pigs go outside to the wolf."

A hinge creaked behind him from the kitchen door. Soft breaths from the phone, waiting. He pictured his little girl tucked under a furry blanket six hundred miles away, green eyes peeking out, the spill of her fine light hair. He pictured her needing him, heaved a deep breath and stepped out into the close cold of the night.

Just get to the truck and out of this creepy place. His keys were in one hand, the phone still raised in the other. A tiny gleam of light reflected off his chrome grille, a hint of red side panel, and he fixed his eyes on it. Just get to the truck. The shoulder of his jacket whispered along the wall of the diner and he jerked away from it.

A small, bright laugh came from somewhere close. He heard it in his ear in the same instant. Rustling ahead, the faint crunch of gravel. When he reached the corner, the vast black space opening before him, he paused and looked up. No moon hung in the endless stars. That one light in the eave of the diner's roof had been holding on, bravely throwing out its white heaven for Forsyth. Now it flickered and winked and was gone.

A Discreet Music

And how can body, laid in that white rush,
But feel the strange heart beating where it lies?

—W. B. Yeats

The dark bloodless taste of widowhood had coated Hiram's mouth for three nights when he awoke alongside that cold gulf of bed. He knew at once some kind of change had visited as he slept. Two hard knots burned in his shoulder blades, and feathers were strewn like bleached leaves across the sheets. But he looked out the window, away from these things, bleary-eyed and trying to miss Sandra.

It had begun to snow in the night, the last of the Virginia winter. By late morning the flurries would turn thick and settle into blankets, bright against the pallbearers' black suits. Bright against his own.

And he was glad it was Sandra he saw through the window and not that other. He drifted into thoughts of his wife, the kind a fresh widower should have, and the bed held him in its half-empty palm. This same oak frame had supported them every night of their forty-two years, the creaks of Sandra rising from it each day the only alarm clock he'd needed. This same shade of pale blue on the walls. Not much had changed their private architecture.

The phone chirred from the nightstand. Sandra's pillow lay plump beside it, the shape of her head already gone. He reached across to answer the call but his hand fell inches short. Instead he made a fist and eased a dent into her pillow, almost pressed his face there to take in the smell of her hair. He couldn't bring himself to give his guilt that satisfaction.

He looked back out the window and watched a handful of years melt from her, Sandra in her dirt-smeared apron, turning the soil around the hellebores with a spade. She climbed to her feet and dragged the back of her hand across her forehead, leaving a red-brown streak that stood out like a brand. And like a brand, it seemed to Hiram the one image of her that wanted to live on for him. Her hair was twisted into a tight silver bun, and he was able to savor, still after all this time, the thought of her undoing it before bed. Her one vanity freed and plunging down her back, anticipating the comb of his fingers. She was always so quick to gasp at his touch.

Now the front yard lined itself with pews, and somewhere close Hiram walked their daughter, Helen, down the aisle, but the window framed only Sandra in blue chiffon, the gold of her hair then only interrupted by subtle ribbons of gray, like guests she had not invited.

But the streak of dirt was on her forehead still, and he thought of her soon in the earth and turned his head away, squeezing his eyes shut. He'd been a smoker until his sixtieth birthday, while she was the one who used the treadmill he'd bought. How had her heart lurched with a fatal thunder while his crept on? A feather brushed his cheek, pulled a teardrop into itself. His shoulder blades ached like something missing.

Gravel crunched in the driveway. Helen had come to take him to the church. He lay there, for a last moment ignoring the dull pain in his back and the feathers scattered across the sheets. Helen had always had a key to the house. Sandra had never accepted that her little girl had long since left the nest, but since she'd only moved an hour away, maybe Sandra hadn't quite been wrong.

The front door opened and Hiram swept the feathers down the bed, yanking the comforter up to his neck just as his daughter rapped on the bedroom door. "Daddy?" she said. "Are you decent?"

Decent. The word rang dull as a wrapped bell. He didn't respond.

Helen came into the room already wearing a gentle exasperation on her face. She held a plastic cleaner's bag, and Hiram didn't want to see the stark black suit inside. He found himself angry that he saw more of himself than Sandra in that face. As if she, too, was not paying her mother the proper tribute. It was his upturned flare of the nose, his dirty blue eyes flecked with green like an algae-stained pond. He only found Sandra in his daughter's cheekbones, the soft jut of the chin, something faint in the shape of her mouth.

"Daddy, I'm sorry but you can't do this," she said. "Not today."

"I'm not feeling well," Hiram whispered. "Maybe tomorrow."

She sat down on the bed. "It's okay that you didn't go to the viewing, Daddy," she said. "Everybody understands. But the funeral is now, not tomorrow. You know that. You have to come say goodbye to her."

He looked out the window again. Only snow falling in vague lines. "Just give me a minute," he told her.

When Helen had hung the suit on the closet door and left the room, Hiram forced himself out of bed. Three or four feathers were caught in his wake and swirled briefly to the floor.

He pulled his t-shirt off. In the mirror his bloodshot eyes regarded him, the skin sagging below them into little troughs. He stalled the moment as long as he could—knowing Helen wouldn't hesitate to knock on this door too—and turned around, twisted his chin back onto his shoulder. Feathers, a dozen or more matching the strange snowfall in the bed, were stuck to his upper back. He plucked one off and a sharp tugging pain brought a hiss through his teeth. It had come *out*, not off. A trickle of blood ran down from the new wound.

He backed a step closer to the sink. Ignoring the feathers, he saw what was more worrisome: something, a growth or tumor, stretched the skin high on each of his shoulder blades. They leaned away from one another, two inches or so wide and half as long, the skin around them pulled taut. He reached, old muscles complaining at the unnatural angle, and touched the one on the left, baring his teeth against a surge of pain that didn't come. It kept the same low ache and was both cool and hot to the touch.

Hiram caught his gaze in the mirror again—wings? The idea felt as foreign as tree roots under his skin, or motor oil in his veins. He denied it, shut it all from his mind. This brought Sandra back into it where she belonged, but just behind her, drawing closer in his return to the foreground, was Jim. He most of all did not want to think of Jim, not today, this ghost that had only now demanded that Hiram admit he was still haunted.

*

He whispered into the casket. Its cherry wood was polished to an unnatural shine, but mercifully the undertaker had been sparing with Sandra. She lay muted and worn and beautiful against the pale satin.

"I'm so sorry, love." Hiram stood there and seemed to feel all those stages of grief upon him, cycling away, each seeking purchase. There was a great weight pressed against him, that she could die when he was the less defensible. Her hands were folded across her chest, and he cupped one of his own over the dry cool skin. He would have felt blessed to crawl into the coffin with her, reach up and pull the lid down over the both of them. He drew his hand away and traced the back of a finger along her jawline. A small white feather slipped from his cuff and into the hair behind her ear. He wondered whether to leave it there.

The mutter of the church built slowly behind him. He turned, his shoulders giving a throb beneath the tight seams of his suit coat. For a moment he didn't see the cousins and the friends gathered there, Helen comforting someone whose head bowed under a cloud of white hair. He saw 1981, the last year they had before Hiram quietly doomed himself with Jim Hudson. He saw one summer night, in a canoe he and Sandra had taken out on Parson Black Lake, the moon a bloated joy hanging up there just for them. He heard the cicadas filling the world, and Sandra whispering, "Let's jump in."

Hiram looked back to his wife. She'd been such a smiler. He closed his eyes and reminded himself it was the funeral, not 1981 and not the viewing, either. He had avoided seeing her like this, and now here he was. He felt Helen's presence as she reached him, and before she could grasp his shoulder, the swollen knot there, he turned and took her warm, thriving hand. Let her lead him to the front pew. He sat and thought of that canoe, set adrift by an oar braced against the tree-crowded bank. He thought of how young his hands had been that night, holding the oar, how clean they had been.

•

"The eye is the first circle." Jim had told him that beside the Missouri River, in the early hours of Hiram's second night in St. Louis. It had always sounded like a quote to Hiram, but in the moment he'd been too embarrassed to ask. The words wouldn't leave his head these past days, so he typed them into Google and learned they were from an Emerson essay. Jim spoke to him all over again as he read. About how the second circle is the horizon seen by the first, and how this shape comes to be repeated through nature and the world, on and on.

He thought about that repetition, outward from the circle of his own vision, first glimpsing the tall black-haired man reaching up to staple a Xeroxed paper to a less-cluttered height of a telephone pole, denim shirt riding up three tanned inches above the thick belt. All those razor-straight horizon lines. The man's sign offered a reward for a lost miniature Pinscher named Otis. Hiram had thought it a kindness, to not cover up the flyers already there. It was the first and last time he ever felt this heat-flash reaction toward anyone. That it was a man disoriented and thrilled him.

They'd shared guilty food and their first guilty kiss under the Arch. Hiram had been sent to Missouri for a week to attend a tech convention, and he wondered how many of the other tourists craning their necks had wives back home. "If that wasn't the gateway kiss, I don't know what is," Jim had told him when their lips pulled apart. They'd held hands through the sparse downtown and let the stares bounce off them. The week had seemed as long as a breath. At the end, the airport, glazed with the awe of what he'd done, he wondered where Otis was. If he'd be found.

Circles. Coming back, always. It was how he had thought about Jim all these years, he realized now, thirty-three of them, thirty-three loops back to the fourth night and a fifth of bourbon in a hotel room. Had the room been on the sixth floor? No, it had been far too dingy a place to stand that tall. There had been a thump and a shout through the thin wall, "Quiet the fuck down." The rattled wheeze of the air conditioner on their sweat-slicked skin. Clenching and pulling, their soft animal sounds. He wondered where that Wild Turkey bottle was now, if it still had the ancient taste of their lips on its mouth, and why was his memory doing this to him?

Sandra had been arranging a bridal bouquet at work when her heart quit on her. She'd gone quickly, the florist blurted out when he called, that strange consolation everyone seemed to fumble for. Hiram had squeezed the phone until its plastic groaned, imagined her on the concrete floor among clipped gardenia stems, her hair come unraveled from its bun and silvering all the vivid color in the shop.

But his second thought, elbowing the first rudely aside, had been of Jim. What Jim might look like now, did he have grandchildren, did they brown in the sun the way he had. The thunderbolt of guilt at that had come, but it had taken a shameful long time.

He remembered all the nights he padded into the bathroom while Sandra slept in her bland peace. His left hand pretending the porcelain ridge of the sink was the corded muscles in Jim's thigh while he thrust himself into the right. The grease spot from his forehead on the mirror as he finished, gritting his teeth against a week that kept falling further into the past. He would stand there so long the covers had cooled when he returned to bed, to stare at the ceiling. These acts had to lead him back somewhere. Surely they did.

And, now, he was thinking of Sandra less and less as the hours pooled in the empty house. He and Helen had argued. She'd wanted to stay another week, get him on his feet and into a routine. Hiram had made her go, just four days after they lowered her mother into the wound in the earth, the day the growths on his back split open and blood-smeared vines reached out. The pain grew teeth then and he knew he couldn't have hidden it from his daughter for long. Advil, salve, nothing helped until he took a weary shower and felt an inexplicable relief once the water hit him.

He was beyond the point of denial—they were wings. Arcing out like snowy antennae from his shoulders, each smooth unfurling feather the length of a hand. They were soft enough for pillows once the blood was washed out and they dried. Another day or two, he sensed, and he could fold them beneath a coat. Afternoons were starting to touch fifty degrees, but still with a thread of ice in the air.

He sat at his desk and scrubbed his face with his hands. He typed "Jim Hudson" into the search bar, and his finger waited for some sign, fidgeting near the keyboard. There would be thousands of Jim Hudsons, his own hiding in their midst, somewhere. Even in an obituary, he warned himself.

"You should stay through the weekend, Hiram Newell," Jim had said that faraway night, and curled his hand into a tube through which he watched him. Then Jim said it again, only this time it meant, *You should stay longer than that.* But Hiram knew he couldn't. The closest he would get was writing one long, anguished letter two years later, then tearing it into smaller and smaller pieces until his fingers cramped.

Jim had reached across the bed for him, and their bodies made a circle. One that had never, for Hiram, gained any circumference. He wondered how he dared dream of protracting it now, in the wake of his wife's death, when his anatomy was occupied with becoming an angel.

An angel—what gave a man the right? He loved Jim. He was surer than ever, now the bottle was uncorked. He tapped enter and began to sift.

•

The wings matured entering the second week. He admired them in his wife's standing mirror, reflecting that he'd never had any particular grace in his life. Sandra had always carried enough for the both of them.

But already they felt an organic part of his body. A bunching of the muscles in his back gave the wings a powerful flex and bloom, as if in warning, mating, or yearning for flight, all of which he was trying to ignore. They spanned six feet at this reach, until the elbowed joints bent and he collapsed them down against his back. Thin, hollow rails of bone extended along the outer edge of each. The feathers stank but he didn't mind, as he now bathed every few hours. His pores thirsted for the comfort of water.

There were moments in which he reveled in the wings. There were moments in which he despaired of them. And in those various moments, either Sandra or Jim. He was delaying both. He'd stopped searching for Jim two days after he'd begun, unable to see how he fit into this new mythology. His wife, or someone of import, wanted him to join her, in heaven, he supposed. Hiram would have to find his own grace now, for angels did great works, lithely, purely.

At last he climbed up on the roof in the tenth night and jumped off. Both wings caught the air but couldn't come close to holding it. He dropped like a stone and heard bones snapping, dry and brittle, the pain red then black. Sometime later he woke shivering on the grass, wet with frost in the building dawn light.

His left wing and arm healed with strange speed. The mild flu he picked up in the damp and the cold faded. The feathers began to spread over his skin just as quickly, emerging down his back and around onto his abdomen. The flightless wings seemed less grand to him now, after the failed attempt at the sky.

And there were other changes to consider. The full head of hair he'd managed to hold onto began to turn white and stiff. A bridge of skin grew between each of his toes. He lay in bed and stared at them, slowly realizing. Slowly accepting. Slowly coming to a decision.

51

He started hearing music while he lay mending. Distant strains of something circling in on itself, simple melodies that he could almost place. It had the quality of a shy transistor radio in the next room. Later, in spring, he might have assumed it was an ice cream truck, trawling some near neighborhood and carrying through the warming air. But this was more discreet, warm and synthesized, and it both calmed and drove him mad from wishing he could turn the volume up, to climb inside its notes.

Three weeks after the funeral, he resolved at last to find Jim. He swung his legs—which were thinning to the bone, the skin shading a charcoal gray—out of the bed. In the gloom of the hall a shape retreated from him, the twirl of a blue skirt as the figure turned into the kitchen. He followed but the room was empty. Sandra's mother's cast-iron skillet swung gently over the stove, as if it had been hung from its hook a moment ago, or touched in passing.

Sandra kept her distance from him. He woke the next few mornings to sense her pressed into a corner of the bedroom, away from the curtains, and when he stood or even looked toward her, she was gone. "What is it you want, love?" he asked. But her old force of personality had departed, or was slow to return.

He checked the mirror with an obsession. No angel he'd heard of was covered in feathers, as he might soon be. A swan, then. He felt certain that his neck would begin to stretch, the feathers continue to flower, and this old ugly duckling would transcend into something more beautiful. Because the symbolism of it—the very thought of it all told him he was meant to be with Jim.

His days settled into the routine Helen had wanted for him. He ate buttered toast at the dining room table and, from the corner of his eye, watched Sandra in her garden. She would only stand and look down at her flowers, hating them or waiting for spring, it was hard to tell. Her hair fell as golden as it had the afternoon he'd coaxed her virginity from her in her grandfather's apple orchard. And, always just behind this image, he thought of that night on the lake, how she'd tried to talk him into the water.

He stopped wearing shirts so the wings could breathe, so the plumage could have its way with him. When his daughter called, she remarked on the brightness in his voice. He sat at the computer through the afternoon into dark. From his home in Charlottesville he placed a virtual pushpin in St. Louis and worked outward, scanning various links and social media accounts for pictures of Jim.

Sandra crept closer during his hours online, until at last she would stand behind him, still only a hint in his peripheral vision watching him work. "I always knew something wasn't right," was the first thing she whispered to him. "When you'd push into me. When I could even get you to."

"Now that's not true, Sandra." He held his face in his hands. "We had forty-two good years."

"Who is Sandra?" Her cold breath soft on his neck. "All I wanted was a man. I wish I'd known that was what you wanted, too." She was gone when he turned.

*

Jim lived west of Philadelphia. Hiram broke down into sobs when he found him, first at the proof that he was alive, and then again just to see him, tall and hale in a crisp blazer. Hiram zoomed in on the photo and touched one pixelated cheek. Beautiful, still beautiful.

Below the picture were two thin paragraphs about Jim's retirement last year as principal of a middle school. Hiram had only stopped working three months before that, and it seemed yet another thing to draw them closer. The article mentioned Jim's eighteen years of service to the children of West Chester, Pennsylvania, his community service work, and that he was looking forward to time with his family. Hiram stared at the word *family*, whispered at it, but it would not give up its secrets.

A few more minutes and he had Jim's phone number and address. Nearly two hundred and fifty miles separated them. Hiram stood and went to the window of the living room. Forsyth Street was a sunshone silence through the half-open blinds. He let his wings unfold to their full span. The feathers had now claimed him from thighs to collarbones, covered him in layers of warm white. His hands ran up and down his body as the empty street aged past noon.

He wept again, with an elaborate, scared joy. Out at the edge of his hearing was that music. It carried the same elegant distance, and he thought it must be the music of the angel he wasn't going to become. Somewhere in the house Sandra was crying, too.

812 Goshen Road. The address was full of harsh consonants, but Hiram relished each one as he tried to decide how to contact him. A letter or email would be the sensible thing after all the years, but even a phone call wasn't enough. Not for this. He already knew he'd drive every one of those five hours in taut electrical suspense, just to see Jim's eyes widen into circles of reunion.

"Did you want both of us?" He felt her murmur in his hair.

"I should have told you all those years ago, love, I should have. But you know, swans mate for life. And I did that. We did that."

"You're a creature now." But she fell silent after these words. Hiram packed an overnight bag, sent Helen an email saying he was going on a little trip and she shouldn't worry. He dressed in his best jeans and loosest shirt, buttoning it to the top to hide his feathers, the wings folded tight inside against his back. Sandra kept her quiet even as he eased himself into the old station wagon.

He bought a pack of cigarettes before he turned onto I-66, and the first one tasted like coming home at the end of a long dark trip, not this lustrous beginning. Every cough that scraped out of him was an old enemy making amends.

＊

"Is this your swan song, Hiram?" Sandra whispered as the car passed north out of Virginia. He could see the suggestion of her in the rearview, in the middle of the backseat with her hands folded on her lap. She might have been smiling with her old half-mirth.

"Just let me have this," he said, and stopped checking the mirror. He'd known her for more than two-thirds of his life, and though her humor could bite, her scorn never had. Pictures of how to approach Jim slid through his mind, but he couldn't seize any of them for scrutiny. When he saw him he would know. He lit his fourth cigarette and rasped at its smoke. His throat was raw.

Just over the Pennsylvania line, he pulled into a rest stop. Sandra stood behind him in the narrow stall as he sat there, his spindly blackening legs cocked out to each side. She chuckled soundlessly. From the stall next to him came the staccato clicking of a cell phone.

"You're a creature now," she whispered again, "a thing for cold water."

"You could be just my guilt," he told her. The clicking of the phone stopped at this pronouncement. "Because why would you haunt me? I loved you. We had a good life." Hiram decided his business couldn't be done here with all this attention. He should just go, get past these last few miles.

"I don't know how I got here." And she was gone, in a way that felt different, like the air had sewn itself back together around his words, where she couldn't fit. The toilet to his right flushed and bright white sneakers passed under the door in front of him. Hiram was left in perhaps true peace.

.

Jim's house was warm and attractive, a brick split-level with a cavernous garage, openmouthed with invitation. The driveway sloped up briefly, so that Hiram couldn't see inside. He rolled the station wagon a half-block forward and parked. His hands trembled. He held them up. They and his face had been spared this transformation, had gotten him here, ostensibly whole. But he sensed the rest of this would come soon.

Cars pulled into other driveways, home from work, and the sun already touched the top of the tree line, pointing shadows across the asphalt toward where Hiram waited. "Get to him while he'll still know it's you," he said to no one, and got out of the car, the old door creaking. His bones creaked with it. His body cried out to be wet.

He stood at Jim's mailbox and heard that same elusive music drifting out of the open garage. His feathers ruffled at it. His heart thrilled along a scale of breathless emotions. All the warmth folded inside the cold evening air seemed to settle upon him.

Hiram walked up to the garage and there Jim stood, reaching to hang a hammer on a wall peg. The sight of Jim's back, his chambray shirt sliding above worn jeans, overwhelmed him. Here was the great circle, of course it was, and at his gasp, Jim turned. Hiram saw all those years pass across his face, furrows deepening along his forehead and around his eyes.

"Hiram?" His voice even richer than the memory of it. The eyes a hue lighter, perhaps. "How in—is that you?"

"It is." Hiram swallowed, tried not to flex his wings

inside his shirt, where they itched to escape. "I just came by to see if you ever found Otis." His smile hurt. He touched his lips and they felt stiff and prominent. There wasn't much time, then. The wonderful music played on, from somewhere in the house.

"Otis? My dog?" Finally Jim stepped toward him, still taller than Hiram by a head, that head as gray as his own had been a month ago. "No, I never found Otis. He just ran off, I guess."

"Like I ran off," Hiram said, and wouldn't let himself look down at the oil stain on the concrete.

Jim grinned. "Yeah, at about the same time, too."

"Well, I came to apologize, Jim. And to tell you things."

"Tell me what things? Wait," he said, and looked past Hiram down to the street with a sigh. "I guess you should come in and have a coffee."

Hiram followed him into the kitchen. He leaned against a counter and watched Jim take two cups down from a cabinet. Still the music was a room away, its tones washing with a kind of mournful hope. "I never was raised with God," he said, a tremor in his voice, "but I had to stay with my wife. I loved her. I don't know how I could love you like I did, the almost terror of it, and still love her. But I found a way, I suppose."

Jim paused with the steel pot over a bright red mug. "Now, Hiram, look." There was a tremor there, too. Hiram heard it shimmer in the middle, in his name.

"When Sandra died I felt—I don't know, but there was a freedom there. And I thought of your circles. You saying the eye is a circle, the first one. I had to—I just had to see you." His fingers fidgeted with his shirt buttons, setting each one loose.

"Hiram." Jim set the pot down on the counter, and the sound it made on the granite was a stark punctuation. "We had something a long time ago, and I still think about you now and again. That's more than I can say about most of the men I've known. But half our lives have passed. I've been with someone for twenty years. He'll be home in half an hour. He's got a fine son who's given us two beautiful granddaughters."

The music hadn't stopped exactly, but Hiram could no longer hear it. "But we're a circle," he said. His fingers opened the next to last button on his shirt.

"You show up after thirty-odd years and expect what from me?" Jim said, looking down toward Hiram's waist. "I asked you to stay, and you didn't. We might've done great things together, but we didn't. It's okay. Not everything circles back. It can't."

Hiram's shirt fell away to reveal his thick vest of feathers. He shrugged it off and the wings burst up toward the low ceiling. "I love you," he said. "I love you," and he stepped toward Jim, cupped a hand on his cheek, and kissed him. He felt the rigid cold of his own lips against the pinched withdrawal of the other man's.

Jim shoved him away and began to speak, but Hiram couldn't hear that either. There was pain in his ears and constricting his face. He saw the white tips of feathers creeping into his field of vision. The room blurred and he ran from the kitchen, through the garage, out of the broken circle.

He sat behind the wheel of the station wagon and wept as night thickened around him, a great urgency rising through the shame and lust. His body throbbed with change. He managed thirty miles south on the highway, until the wings shifted forward and began to take his arms into them, bone knitting into bone. An exit sign loomed and he turned right, coasting down the ramp and grinding the car to a stop on the rutted shoulder.

His neck elongated as he staggered out. His torso bunched into itself, down and back onto his legs. He felt his lips peel outward, fuse together with his nose, and he let the resulting protuberance, a creamy red-orange, point him along the exit.

The surf of traffic noise continued behind him. Lights winked from a gas station down the road. Trees swallowed the rest. At last spring was returning to earth, even this far north. An irrepressible warmth moistened the dark. Time receded from him and he was compelled after it, into the wood full of black oaks and cedars and white pines. Sound came back to him, but the machinery and murmur of the world had somehow fallen away here. There was only the crackle of his shifting bones.

Hiram ached for his two great loves. He longed for Jim but wept more for his wife. She was the one who had kept him. He wished he could resign himself to her all over again. What Jim had told him back in that kitchen was right, but then where was the circle Hiram had spent half his life tracing? What did this transformation ask of him?

He was still endlessly in the forest when dawn threaded through the canopy of crosshatched branches, and the same muted hush coated the world like dew. At last he broke through into a wide and round clearing, within which was held a pond, a nearly perfect circle, its circumference marred only by a tongue of shore penetrating the water. Sandra sat on this tongue, or someone did. Thick bands of dirty light fell upon her there, and her hair shone gold inside of them. A spade jutted from the earth at her feet.

He walked over to the rim of water and looked down at what he had become. Wondrous and graceful and hideous, the long curved neck drooping to witness his culmination. He stood perhaps four feet high with his head bowed. The feathers had long finished colonizing him. Black pebble eyes regarded the beaked head cocking to the left. He reached to touch his face and realized again that his arms had gone. In their place the wings gave an undecided jerk before settling back along his sides.

"Let's jump in," a voice said. A strong dawn voice. He turned and it was not Sandra, had never been, but a young woman, her fine hair falling around her face. No longer a trick of the eye, she grew more firm and full the longer he looked at her.

Hiram worked his way out of what little of his clothes remained. His feet were black fans stretched around his toes. He leaned over and dipped his head into the water, cold as heaven and clearer than heaven could have been. The urge to ride this still mirror rose fierce in his gullet, but he withdrew his head and shook the droplets free. Dozens of circles radiated on the pond's surface.

He turned to her again. "Who are you?" His voice had grown reedy and flat, vibrations traveling along a papery membrane. But they were words he spoke.

"I don't know how I got here," the young woman said, turning to him. "But the water looks so nice, doesn't it?"

He moved toward her. Behind, the sun began to spill more generously into the bowl of trees, and the crooking shape of Hiram fell over the woman. Pictures of Sandra and Jim clenched his stomach in dark hunger, but soon their faces began to drift apart and become the one he now looked upon. He thought of his daughter, and his dismay at Helen fading in his mind likewise faded after her. The circles were getting smaller. The ripples were calming.

"Yes," he answered the woman, this buxom thing that had recently stepped fresh out of girlhood. The supple face flushed with life, the streak of dirt on her forehead, all darkened beneath him. She wore a green, crimped smock and a sheer night-blue skirt, which to Hiram appeared to be tented with a man's swollen desire. He stared at the erection and said, "Is this place where the music comes from?"

"It's there." She looked across the water. "You just don't hear it now. You are a god of want."

"What is your name?" His new heart beat in his new breast upon her coming response. Her milk thighs unclasped. She looked delicious inside his shadow, and he shifted closer, as though to taste her.

She half-smiled up at him from her perch, a quiver in her soft wet lips as she answered.

The Devil Under the Maison Blue

Gillian notices that no one ever closed Mr. Elling's attic window. A week has passed since the brief swirl of ambulance lights near dawn. Already his house seems decades older.

She's staring across at it when she hears his voice say, "Lord, child, you about run as far as you can get." He has a rich and rumbly cadence. There's a crackle in it, too, faint as a needle at the end of one of his records. Somehow she is not startled, though he might as well be perched right here beside her, on the high sharp peak of her house. That's how close his words are; she feels them in the shingles under her hands, and in the cups of her ears.

She sees him (for a second she's sure of it) in his old chair, rocking slowly toward and away from her, in and out of the pool of a hanging bulb. Even from a distance he looks ancient, his skin like dried dates. The silver of his hair glints and fades. She can't see his eyes, but she pictures them, heavy-lidded, stained the yellow of a smoker's teeth.

He was the only person she could talk to in her six

months here, though most days she'd just listen. Stories about his life in the big jazz towns; who played what with whom before when. He could talk the sun down, tapping the valves of his battle-tarnished trumpet idly in his lap. Betty, he called the old horn, with something in his voice that said she was his one true love. His lungs couldn't handle her anymore, but sometimes, just to get a smile, he'd lift her up and blow his cheeks out into great globes. Then cough a while after.

For the first time she wonders if maybe he knew that listening would do her more good. Her father pulled her out of school after the day in the maple trees. No way she could have gone back in September, and so the summer stretched out toward winter in one long, opaque strand. Now Mr. Elling's words carry clear through the space between their houses like the few stray starlings (they're late flying south) calling to one another above. Like the birds, no one sees her when she's up here. Faraway cars on the highway sound like the ocean. She can pretend the starlings are gulls and she is somewhere else, a place that, if only for a little while, doesn't have her father in it.

She calls across asking Mr. Elling if he is a ghost. He breathes a deep sigh. "You just hush," he says. "No need for you to be yelling. It don't much matter what I am. I ain't haunting nobody, that's for sure. Just lingering. I got a story I kept letting myself not tell you. Before, it was a story about my daddy and me. Now it's maybe got room for you and yours, and that's a terrible thing to come to."

A minute unravels. She listens to the birds. "Look at that sky, Gillian," he says. She has to grip the shingles, so wide and heavy is the shock of hearing that. To Mr. Elling they're just words. He says them kindly, like another sigh, but she remembers (she's always thinking of) the backseat of her father's convertible after a sudden detour into a clump of maples, her mouth still sticky from ice cream. Her father whispered those words and then sneaked a kiss along her neck, as she peered up between the full trees, into blind blue and clouds like stuffing pulled out of dolls.

Today's sky is much the same, a little whiter. The clouds hang closer. Someone is burning leaves, but not nearby. She presses her hand to her belly, cold against the tight warmth there.

"I will surely miss this northern sky," Mr. Elling says, and makes a close-mouthed little "mmhm" sound before he goes on. "But one last story before I move on to wherever it is I'm headed. Betty and me had us some good years, and I'm satisfied.

"See, the best times were bebop, hard bop, all the bops. The birth of the cool. I'm lucky those times were the ones I happened to be in. The greats slipped on more new styles than a woman in a shoe store. They always were looking for the next big groove, the next big rule-breaker. And you might ask how a brokedown young fella from South Carolina with a drunk waste of a daddy could bus hisself down to Louisiana, with just a dream in his head of playing with actual *gods*. Well, there's a reason us old folks get to say we were young once."

The handful of starlings has fallen quiet. Nothing moves through his attic window now, if anything ever did. She can almost pick out the last few patches of red paint on the rocking chair's pale arms. She can come close to riding the swells of his voice, the pop and hiss of a well-worn tune.

"But piss on all that history lesson talk," Mr. Elling goes on. "You don't know the insides of jazz aside from my jawing, but just know that folks like Coltrane and Monk—never Miles, wasn't nobody blowing trumpet beside that man and not coming off like a bugler in a doomed infantry—they were reason enough to sell your soul."

And for a moment, just one, she seems to hear her mother singing Billie Holiday under her breath, seems to see her far below (in a yard she never knelt in) trimming back the row of holly. As though both of Gillian's important ghosts are here. She seems to smell her, too, not the powdered lavender of her hugs but something that traces her mother's freckled skin further down in her mind: honeysuckle, like the vines that spread wild in the woods behind the old neighborhood, before the hospital, before the house went dusty and full of echoes and she and her father moved away. To here.

And she almost says that, yes, she does know the insides of jazz.

Mr. Elling's old voice takes on the weight of memory. "Like I told you a time or three, I came to the Big Easy late in the game. It was a frying-pan August, 1958, about as humid as humid gets. Beautiful city, crumbling slow and majestic. Green growing on everything. The day I got there my precious mama was in her grave just shy of three weeks and my daddy wasn't worth the dirt in it.

"I could play a mean trumpet, had been since I was fifteen until my daddy put a stop to it. And I had big plans to travel around, looking up at my name in tall letters on marquees. But I was a beanpole with the lungs to match. I didn't have the soul of the greats. Betty and me got to perform with some guys exactly twice between then and October of '59. That night was set to be my third, as I'd just started making some regular friends by then, something like a crew. Strictly small-time, but it was better than *no*-time, if you catch my drift.

"Except thirty feet outside the back door of the Maison Blue, on Frenchman Street, I met myself four and a half white fellas all liquored up and looking for somebody like me—the biggest one I'm counting as a fella and a half. I didn't know them from Adam, and they didn't know me from whoever was the first black boy in the Bible. Well, suffice it to say I never stepped foot in the Blue that night. Later I found out a kid called Rett Wilson sat in for me. Not half bad for a tin ear. He did some session work on a few records.

"Excuse an old-timer, Gillian. I never told this story before, but that's no excuse for all my other recollections to come seeping in the cracks. Even passed on I may be longwinded, but I mean to get through this quick, so that we can see what we see."

He laughs and there's not a drop of wheeze in it. And no humor, either. She watches for the faded bronze of her father's old Cabriolet. Her hand rubs nervous circles on her belly.

"I don't know what I had more of on me," Mr. Elling says, "blood or dirt. I made quite a dust cloud in that back lot, what from hitting the ground over and over. Them fellas left, brushing off their white, white shirts. I could see two of my teeth right in front of my eyes, and judging from the inside of my mouth I figured there were probably a few more scattered around. My Betty, I could just see her down by my feet. She was streaked with some red, too.

"One of my eyes was already swelled shut, but the other one saw something gleaming at me from the crawlspace under the Blue. Flashlight eyes, like a cat. There was a little door dragged open along the dirt, and they were staring out from the black square behind it. I could feel my busted ribs and I was spitting out blood so I didn't drown in it. That is, I was fine where I was; at some point somebody would step out back for some air and fetch me to the hospital.

"But damned if those eyes didn't get bigger and yellower. Damned if they weren't looking at me with something deeper than a cat's cool regard. Then they pulled back into that dark, lamps trailing off down a mine. Might be the cat's supposed to be the curious one, but that long evening it was me.

"Most folks wouldn't have gone hauling themselves through the dirt toward that hole, grinding broken parts inside with every inch. Most folks would've passed out from the pain of it, and in that way, I was most folks. But I came to and I crawled some more, and when I made it to that black opening, I peered in, smelling sour dirt and cool dark."

She almost tells him she's on the edge of her seat—this would get a laugh out of him, ghost or no—but she keeps quiet. The street is empty and breathless, the sun sliding on its track, closer to the line of coloring trees.

"But I supposed that was no cat. Just like I supposed if I squeezed into that hole, it would be like no dark I ever saw. So I went on ahead and did it. There was a lot inside me that wasn't doing so hot; them white boys had wanted to beat me within an inch of life, and they measured good. Stands to reason they knocked something loose in the clear thinking part of my head.

"About the second my feet were inside, the door scraped shut behind me. The ceiling wasn't two feet above my head. I couldn't hear even a floorboard creak from inside the Blue. It was like climbing into my own grave.

"And I felt something come right up to my face in that pitch dark. It felt bigger than the Maison Blue itself. I went cold all over. I was already in shock, if not from the beating then for sure from dragging my cracked self across the Blue's lot and through that hole.

"'What do you want?' I asked the blackness, and it came right back with a silence that stretched out like a line of mountains way off in the distance. I held my breath and heard my heart."

His own voice trails off much the same way—Gillian knows the Adirondacks are out there, past her eyes around the curve of the earth—and now she sees the convertible, black canvas top up for the cold season, slide down the street to her left. It pulls into their driveway, earlier than most days. Her father steps out and gazes up at the roof, his head tipped back. The house is tall and skinny, so unlike her; at

68

more than thirty feet up, it's easy to pretend she doesn't hear him call her name.

"Well, speak of the devil," Mr. Elling says, and this time there is some shine to his laugh. Again she almost sees his hands gripping the chair, ticking back and forth in time with her heartbeat. Those hands he would always describe as coffee up top, cream on the bottom.

"I thought I was messing with something bad under there, something *biblical*, but I was a long way off from being too old to make a boy's mistakes, if ever a man is. To go looking for trouble. So I told the dark, 'I want to be one of the greats.' I was flat on my stomach from having to worm inside that thin space, so can you blame me? I had already assumed a worshipping position. 'I want Betty and me to travel the world and sit in with the giants and to see their eyes like dinner plates when they hear me play.'

"Back then most folks, myself included, hadn't ever heard the story of Robert Johnson, him cradling his old guitar at the crossroads, the devil holding out a heap of genius in exchange for his soul. He'd been dead going on twenty years, but his brand of fire and blues hadn't caught on yet. I hadn't ever heard of Faust and his bargain, neither, so mercy knows what got that idea in my head that night, that old Satan was crouched up in the dirt looking to add one more soul to Hell. I suppose I just wanted to play the trumpet that bad. I laid there in that crawlspace, waiting for fire to light it up, and I knew I'd see a hole gaping in the world, and an oily goat-skinned man. Big perfect square teeth and eyes blacker in the flaming light than I'd ever be. He'd drip all colors on the ground and I'd choke on musk thick in my nose.

"But that quiet just went on and that dark kept pressing against me. I had no business still being conscious so I slept a while."

Mr. Elling falls silent, waiting and watching. Gillian's

father climbs out the attic window and sits beside her, still in his suit, checkered tie loosened at his throat. One hand is full of wildflowers tied with string. She stares at his other hand, the one that wastes no time dropping onto her thigh, then peeks over at the sculpted beard on his cheeks, the wiry eyebrows, the hair turning winter at his temples.

A fresh sheet of wind carries again the scent of honeysuckles. A summer smell in the fade of November, a smell from before she came here and she was still allowed to be just a girl with scabbed knees and tangled hair, ranging the woods behind the house she was born in. A girl who had friends at school and a living mother whose arms she could tuck herself beneath.

"I wish you wouldn't come out here, sweetheart," he says. His fingers squeeze, relax.

Her father does not smell of the grave, or the dark under Mr. Elling's jazz club. He is cinnamon gum and aftershave curling through the sweetness of the honeysuckle. When Gillian was little her favorite part of bedtime was the tickle test. She always lost and begged him to stop, but he was one of those people who are only ticklish sometimes. The man beside her now is calm and king of his world. Five months ago he didn't stop. He panted as he pushed her dress up around her waist.

Since that day in the backseat, she can't run through the woods, trying to keep ahead of her beating, squishing heart. There are no woods anymore. Behind the new house are only more houses, boxing her in at each turn. She can't bury her face in a wild flush of honeysuckle vines like she used to, before, when her mother's chemo was at its worst and her father began coming into her bedroom in the evenings. When it was still just his calloused hands, his thin lips emerging from the nest of beard, wanting to be fed.

"You're in a delicate condition," her father says, and gives her the flowers. They smell of nothing.

She looks at him again. Fear and love like the two halves of the gold heart hanging around her neck.

"Some places in the light," Mr. Elling says, "are worse, Gillian." Her father doesn't hear. His face remains soft and his hand kneads and slides. "You're up in the sky but you'd be better off in the dirt under the Blue with the devil you don't know. Fortunately for you, child, I got a tune that was never pressed on no wax."

And now she does see the old man. She sees him lift the trumpet up, the sun flashing off the brass as he brings it to his lips. The chair rocks once, twice, then comes to a stop, the lined face in shadow. And she hears him play, really play, for the first time.

Her father's head turns toward the sound, eyes squinting. The horn comes wafting across, clean and bright, and it's hardly music, she's never heard anything that serves as a point of reference. There are many-petaled syllables, there are quick snaps like sheets on a clothesline in the wind.

"Pretty, isn't it?" she says, and pats the slim space between her and her father. "Here, scooch closer to me." He grins and shifts over, the tacky grit pulling at his slacks. His hip touches hers; his hand drops back down, higher this time, at the crook where her legs join in reluctant heat. And the horn slips into an impossible key, slow notes clouding the air. The two of them gasp as one, only this time he does not gasp in release; nor is her own in tearing pain.

Maybe the atoms of the fall day tremble. They seem to. Briefly, everything is more, the roof slanting up to her like vast, brooding hands, the distant ocean cars full of unwritten stories.

Except her father. He looks so small up here.

For the first time in shameful weeks she aches to have her mother back. She aches even for the glances she'd catch toward the end, as though his fingerprints stood out on her skin like brands. She aches for another chance to sit by her hospital bed, to drape the sheaves of her hair across her mother's (their neighboring shades of rusty orange) and translate the emotion that turned her head away on the pillow.

Gillian's father leans close and breathes into her ear, "It's beautiful. Just like our new family."

Mr. Elling's cheeks go on blowing a mournful joy between his house and hers. The sun rubs the trees and Betty sours, her tone darkening. Her father rests his head against her face; his eyelashes are wet. The halves of her heart gain dreadful weight.

The trumpet dips and rises and cuts out. Mr. Elling says to her, not even having to catch his breath, "That next morning I came out from under the Blue streaked with dirt, Betty tucked beneath my arm. And you know what came traipsing out of that hole with me? A mangy old tabby cat, ordinary as daylight. She glanced at me, licked herself a minute, and went off to find breakfast.

"Later on I'd wonder if the devil had been anywhere near New Orleans that night. And I ain't saying God Himself came down from on high and slithered into that grave beneath the Blue, getting dirt under His fingernails just for me. I haven't ever been able to say that. But it sure feels closer to the truth, somehow. I was all mended up, you see. My back popped as I bent and touched my toes. I ran my tongue across every single one of my teeth.

"And right then I felt I'd given up my soul. I could feel that empty space in me, all hollowed out. Even so, I didn't go seeking fortune and fame, no, not then. I didn't even touch lips to Betty quite yet. I never would go white fella hunting, neither. I put myself on a bus back to South Carolina, and I went to see my own daddy."

She wishes her father would jump. She waits for it, her fingers clenched tight upon the peak of the roof.

"You need to realize," Mr. Elling says, "that your daddy

ain't going nowhere on his own. Folks like him never do, and I can't help you there. Betty had something special in her, but she never had no magic, bless her heart. For a minute, though, riding on that bus, I just knew she did."

Her father kisses the hinge of her jaw. She feels his mouth smile.

"Now my mama was a proud, good woman," Mr. Elling says, and there are rough edges in his voice. "The kindest mother a boy could want. She was in the ground hardly a year by then, and my daddy's fists was mostly the reason she was there. And he still walked his little piece of earth, or he did those rare days he wasn't curled up in drink.

"It was surprising cool in Greer when I stepped off that Greyhound. I found him snoring in his bed. I stood over him and me and Betty played him something awful. And we played him something sweet. By the time the sun set on us, he was hanging from the big oak behind the house. I sat on a patch of dirt and watched him twitch and swing. That patch had been scrubbed clean from years of my feet scuffing it, the times I'd sit listless on my old tire swing, hearing my mama cry through the kitchen window. The light painted my daddy in blood and I wasn't happy, but I wasn't sad, neither, no ma'am."

She waits (look at that sky) but her father does nothing. The horn cries out again, only for a beat, and then bleeds into silence. In the distance she expects a wet coughing to start up in its place, but of course Mr. Elling's lungs aren't clogged with age anymore. They are reborn.

And under her palm, Gillian feels the baby kick. The strangeness of it pulls the air from her.

"Now here's where the deal gets sweet," Mr. Elling says. "There is no deal. All a child's got to do is pick up the telephone, and your daddy will face the music, same as mine. I didn't do nothing except pass on and play you a tune. You were a good friend to an old man these last

73

months. But you don't have to be in that story I told. What you want to do is yours to want, and you ain't got to give me or God a thing. Being happy sure would be nice, though."

She turns to her father for a long moment. "Do I look pretty from down there?" she asks, and points down to the lawn, as perfectly trimmed as his beard. Her face is full of heat. The baby kicks again, demanding to be known.

"Of course you do, honey." He smiles inside the beard. "You look just like your mother."

Gillian places her hand against his side. He leans over and kisses her ear, breathes cinnamon fog into her hair. She gently digs her fingers into the meat of him. He giggles for a bare second, twisting away, and then he's gone. By the time she hears the mundane thump on the ground, she's already watching the sky stain at the edges. The air is still flushed with that misplaced summer sweetness. The tree line, the sinking sun, the starlings blur in her eyes.

There's a wink of light across the way, the silver of close-cropped hair and the battered gold of Betty. Mr. Elling lifts her in a wave, says, "Thing about music is in the end, all we can do is face our own. I hope yours has some bop to it." He steps away into his dark. The chair slows and stills.

She raises her own hand for a second. Below her is silence. She knows she should get inside. There's a bundle of shingles she saw once in the garage. They'll need to be dragged up to the attic and opened up. There's a pouched belt heavy with hammer and nails that will buckle around her father's waist. A tearful phone call to make, a swirl of ambulance lights, before she can at last return to her own narrow bed in her own narrow room.

She knows she should get inside. But she goes back to rubbing the curve of her belly in quiet, calming circles.

October Film Haunt:
Under the House

Alem

The opening shot of *Under the House* lingers from the rim of the tree line for more than two percent of its running time. Lens glare winks pink-yellow, dust motes swell into globules, and beyond the meadow of chest-high grasses, shadows lose their corners in the lowering dusk. It is a fine, if incongruous, tone of introduction.

The four men, believing the film to be incomplete, came to finish it. They stood at this first vantage, taking in the old colonial while the white pines rustled at their backs, squirrels barking up in the branches. Somewhere out near Cord Lake loons answered in the voices of young wolves. The two dogs perked their ears at the calls, then went back to nosing the ground, an uncharted land flush with new scents, wandering into the grass until Cheung and Mayne ordered them back.

The house looked as though it had once shrugged and then gone to sleep, and in that sleep it especially struck

Alem as familiar. And not simply from the film. It was the taste of the air, the way the frame of sky shifted when a sporadic wind caught the treetops. It felt like a place he was going to visit, which didn't make sense, because of course they were here. Why else? Familiar or no, from the end of its overgrown meadow, the windows of the house didn't stare back with any dumb avidity. They didn't resemble eyes at all. Alem found the effect more muted than Lecomte had filmed it, even as he felt the too-perfect anticipation of the curls of old paint peeling from the walls against his palm.

While the others had lost count of their viewings, Alem had been an *Under the House* virgin until the past week. He couldn't believe such a cult classic, however unorthodox, had slipped his radar for so long, and he was still processing what he'd seen. What he was seeing now. A reconciliation of the two. He only knew for certain that the house looked tired, as anything abandoned in the woods would, particularly when seen through no more than the lenses of his contacts.

They were all exhausted. 1,100 miles north to New Hampshire without stopping for a hotel, and Alem in particular wasn't much of a car sleeper.

"Not all that creepy," Harlan said from beside him.

"But see the ring in the grass?" Cheung pointed out into the meadow yard.

"Yeah," Harlan replied. "Hard to miss. Hasn't even grown over much."

"You expect it to be?" Cheung said. "Number one, it was burned there. And number two, the Lecomtites keep it landscaped according to the third scene."

"There's no such thing as Lecomtites," Mayne said. "You need a legacy before you can have any -ites."

Cheung laughed and moved forward into the grass. He was the tallest—Harlan seemed to call him Yao Ming a lot—and the stalks parted around his waist. His golden retriever, Baily, trotted into the fray beside him. Mayne's dog, a border collie, broke his vigil and followed. Apparently Mayne named all his rescues Foster and tried to get their eventual adopters to let it stick.

Alem knew maybe three pieces of trivia about each of these guys. Not much of it helped him form any picture aside from the ubiquitous *horror nerd*. A term he had lately grown to flaunt himself, but somehow these men didn't wear it well. They were a shade too lumberjacky, however beardless. But they were serious, if nothing else. He'd only heard of the October Film Haunt blog this past winter, and meeting Cheung and Harlan at a con in Atlanta had led him, gradually, into the group.

Mayne stepped forward, too, but didn't enter the meadow. The ring was twenty or so feet across, like a crop circle in shorthand. The grass within it reached taller than it did without, in vague monument to something. Cheung was swallowed up by it as he passed through the ring's circumference. He gave a whoop and the others saw his fists peek out in victory.

Alem swiped his lips with the back of a hand. It crossed his mind to leave, already, not even five steps out of the woods. This was his first film haunt. He'd done ghost meetups before, almost since the day he moved to the States. He even spent the night in the small morgue of an abandoned children's asylum once. For an hour he'd tried to sleep on a morgue tray, canned inside the old refrigerated cabinet, until the close dark made him kick the door open. Dust, a sore back, and a story to embellish with Beth, who'd made him shower twice before she let him touch her.

He wasn't sure how this felt different, if it was the possibility of lurking "Lecomtites" or the sense of next-level he got from these three guys. The house itself—he'd tapped into enough of the film's vibe to know he'd rather not go into that basement. And he knew the genre, naturally, and knew not to judge a haunted house by its cover. It hit him that he was acting the cliché, the proverbial disbelief cut with a stirring of unease. He had to smile at himself a little.

One of the dogs yelped a single time, and the grass swayed inside the circle. Mayne ran into the meadow, but Foster had already rocketed away from the group. Alem watched the vague path left in the wake of the dog's panic, toward the house, just like it had happened with the stray dog in the film. Mayne called after the collie again as it disappeared around the back. The grass stilled and Cheung stepped back through the ring.

Alem's unease grew two shades darker. Dogs couldn't reenact scenes. They couldn't be taught to do that, could they? Harlan turned to him and said, "You coming?" Alem put some thought into it—the image of that dark hole at the end of the film both too curious and too atavistic in his mind—before nodding.

The four of them, with Baily in tow, approached the house in near silence but for the lab's faint whimpering. The last few crickets sang out from the woods, and a single squirrel carried on with its determined chatter. Even looming before them, the house was still just a structure, the slow sloughing of gray paint, the white posts grown weary under the sagging porch. Four steps led up to overturned rocking chairs and a heavy mahogany door, above which was nailed a small board with the words *Beloved Mouth* etched across the plain wood. Each glanced at the plaque and turned away as though he hadn't seen it. Alem found this a curious reaction even as he did the same himself. He placed a hand against the wall. His skin hummed for an instant, and a strip of paint broke off in his palm.

"I should go look for Foster," Mayne said, and the others nearly jumped.

"Foster will find us inside," Cheung said, smiling, "if it's like the movie."

"If it's like the what?" Mayne shook his head. "Come

on, man. And the dog in the film wasn't even one of their dogs. It was just there."

"Oh, so you *do* think it's real?" Cheung said, but Mayne didn't reply.

Harlan had told Alem, before they pulled up *Under the House* on YouTube the weekend before, that though Mayne was the biggest geek in the group, Cheung was their believer. Cheung thought that Lecomte wasn't a filmmaker at all, that the movie was just a document of an initiation. Into a cult? Maybe, or just a great puzzle.

Mayne stared up at Cheung for a minute, some fresh tension that hadn't been there earlier, then turned to the door and pushed it open. Dust sifted out into the failing light. They stepped inside.

"The kitchen's where your dog will be," Cheung said. "Stay close, Baily." At some point he'd taken his bag from Harlan, but made no move to remove the small camera. Filming had been a point of contention the entire drive up here, and they'd crossed the New Hampshire line before they all started to admit to the appeal of finishing the film. "Lecomte did the living room first, then dining room and kitchen. We've seen all that."

"You mean where the basement door is," Alem said. There might have been a headache imminent—he had the faint sense of double vision in his memory. Cheung was right, after all—he'd seen this on a laptop screen already.

Cheung ignored him and walked off. The others followed him through the first two rooms, the former containing only a mold-haunted couch that would soon disintegrate into the filthy floor. A long table with a single chair dominated the latter. Dust everywhere. Several thin black cables lay on the floor of the dining room, naked without anything to connect to. There was a small hole at the base of the wall. Alem stooped to see a modem lined with five green eyes, one of which was blinking at him.

"Guys," he said, "there's a—a modem in the wall. It's on."

"A modem?" Cheung said. "Like there's internet here? And to think we didn't even bring our phones." He smiled, silently referencing an October Film Haunt rule.

"But who the hell has this place wired for lights, much less Netflix?" Mayne dragged a palm across the table, and his hand came away furry with dust.

No one had an answer except to try the few light switches they could find. Nothing worked except that hidden modem. After a moment it occurred to Alem that something else was missing: the detritus of the bored or the homeless. No used condoms, no beer cans, no makeshift blanket beds anywhere in the house so far, much less a mattress. Signs of occupancy contradicted signs of complete isolation.

Then the kitchen, and the blank dog.

"Under *Under the House*," by Charles Mayne
Posted on www.filmhaunt.com, September 2015

There is no sound apart from ambient background in *Under the House* until sixteen minutes in, when dark has grown full. Only the creak of doors and floorboards can be heard during the pass through the ground floor, and when the crew finds the dog by the basement door, even then they don't say a word, presumably struck silent. You realize you haven't heard so much as a human breath yet. Not until the film abruptly cuts to outside in the meadow. A healthy campfire fills the frame, a crosshatch of broken limbs billowing smoke. Knots pop. Far away, loons cry their flutelike calls. Then the camera swings higher, past the silhouettes of treetops, to show the smoke-blurred stars, and someone—fans argue whether it's Lecomte—muses into them. It is the only extensive piece of dialogue in the film.

"Some of those stars have hung in the firmament longer than my father did. Swollen things. I can remember one night, the pockmarked moon, riper and younger then. My father had already fallen out of the sky, and soon I would plant him. The world was deeply cold and quiet and I was naked, hugging myself as my bare feet slipped on the surface of the frozen lake. Through those trees there. The third or fourth time I fell my cheekbone cracked against the ice, and I lay shivering, feeling my face go numb even as it puffed up in black pain. Under me the ice was opaque, dusted white, and would not reflect the stars.

"And my father walked beside me, heavy warm boots crunching the scrim of snow, a blanket draped over his arm. Telling me how the stars ate boys like me. His great mouth moved toward my face. Thus began the depth of my education. Trees came and gathered shoulder to shoulder. They walled the lake in tight, and I dwindled to almost a grain in the bowl they made. I only feel large, now, inside this dead grass."

For some reason, the other crew members laugh at this. The camera lowers, to expose them around the fire, and the yellow shaking stalks of grass around the men. Somehow it all isn't swept into a roar of flame. In the seven years since *Under the House* surfaced online, this segment has probably been the most discussed outside the titular scene. The nearby lake is glimpsed later, but the fire in the meadow is the only significant part of the film staged outdoors, and it is considered the pivot point.

The blond man stares across the fire at the camera—or at Lecomte, who is never seen in the film—and says, "*De cette façon, tous nos père ont la meme yeux.*"

They all shift then and gaze toward the camera. No one speaks for the next eleven minutes, they just stare out of your screen at you, and the fire pops and stands swaying in the foreground. A single loon cries once in all that wilderness of silence.

At last the longhaired man looks down into his lap and begins to weep. "Jesus," he says, "is that French, Humley? What's that mean? No way you speak French, do you?" Soon Humley and the balding man, too, are weeping. Bewildered, not knowing why. The camera, presumably held by Lecomte, takes it all in, tripod-stoic and still.

Then the dog, the stray brindled pit bull mix, steps into the frame, the wooden crown and thick ropes of drool hanging from its mouth. Static rains across the screen. Then Humley unfolds himself and staggers off into the night, screaming. Things devolve from there.

Harlan

Foster had been by the basement door, after all, and Harlan wasn't sure what freaked him out more, the slack-faced vacancy of the collie or the mirroring of the film. They found the dog shivering, a puddle of urine spreading in three branches around his front paws. Mayne patted his knees and called Foster to him, but the dog just stared ahead, a line of pasty foam around his mouth. Harlan found himself drawn to the basement door, afraid he might start drooling himself. Finally they gave up and left Mayne with the dog, his voice becoming more and more desperate. They went back outside and entered the ring in the grass, where at some point they started arguing about whether or not to build a fire. Surely this whole place would kindle in seconds if they did. Underneath, Harlan thought, they were debating whether Lecomte was some kind of black magician.

"There wasn't a fire last time," he said. The first traces of steam plumed out with the words.

"Last time?" Alem waved a hand in front of Harlan's face. "We watched the movie just the other day, dude. Campfire burning."

Cheung, the still-unused camera in its bag hanging from his shoulder, swore at the other two when he was outvoted. He refused to acknowledge the swath of dry woods surrounding them, and grass as brittle as newspaper waiting to carry fire into the trees.

So they settled down on the cold earth, the old fire bones between them. A loon called out from much closer than the lake. Cheung played with his lighter, like a reminder to the rest of them, and Baily wouldn't wander more than a foot from his side and preferred to crawl up into his lap when he'd let her.

At one point Cheung looked up at the sky and began to quote the bit about the lake from the film, but was quickly told to stop. Silence fell as they waited for the crown.

"Under *Under the House*," by Charles Mayne
Posted on www.filmhaunt.com, September 2015

The thing is, *Under the House* is a short film. It's only forty-two minutes long. When one considers that over a quarter of those minutes are given to that interminable firelit silence directed at the viewer, it's clear the film is trying very hard to avoid being a straightforward production. When a character says, "In this way, all our fathers have the same eyes" in beautiful, flowing French he supposedly doesn't know, those eyes can hardly be directed toward Hollywood. Or even film school.

Online comment threads still intermittently fume over whether there was supposed to be more to it than that. If *Under the House* in fact *is* a film. The characters are not given an introduction, much less the skeletons of character arcs. The lack of dialogue is even more troubling when one considers there is no discernible story for conversation to push forward. Some say it possibly was intended to have the structure of a typical ninety-minute running time and is therefore unfinished, while others—most—fiercely deny this.

These others point to blatant discrepancies in the film as proof of a complete, edited, deliberate product. Particularly the final thirteen minutes and their jumble of disturbing, nightmarish images. For example, when Humley (the only one other than Lecomte identified in any way) lurches to his feet before fleeing, it seems he is wearing the wooden crown. The static and warping of the video make it a difficult task, but the distinct long tapers of the crown can be seen above his head if the film is paused at the right moment. But clearly the crown is still clenched in the mouth of the unnamed dog, which has just entered the frame. The red sneakers that are seen descending the cellar stairs near the end are identical to the ones the balding man (referred to as variations of "Bald" in discussion of the film) has on, and yet "Bald" is already in the cellar with the others, turning toward the stairs. How to explain those shoes, and how to explain the newcomers at all, for that matter? The film certainly does not. Elsewhere, starting with the appearance of the crown, the faces of the members of the group are at times smudged or blurred in a rudimentary fashion—whether through software trickery or something more sinister is yet another line of contention. It is hard to find any thread of reason in those last minutes.

Compounding all of this is its truncated ending, which has further ensured that no one can come to an agreement on the whole of it as fiction or documentary. Each side has a reasonable argument. One can take its constituent elements aside and easily claim it's all made up with the aid of effects, sure. But snip *The Blair Witch Project* at the right moment— say, forty-two minutes in—and it might easily be construed as a documentation of A Thing That Happened.

It's hard to guess what Lecomte had in mind, or what the environment had in mind for him. *Under the House* is the only thing he ever made, at least as Lecomte. As outré as it is, there is nothing remotely like a filmography out there attached to that surname. Today an internet search will take you through dead ends of fake Twitter handles and message streams. The video simply showed up on a subreddit thread one day in 2008, four million YouTube hits and a few urban legends ago.

But this would all seem to lead back to the same question: Why does this film exist? And almost as importantly, why was it edited in such a way and uploaded to the world with only one word of introduction—"real"—alongside the name "lecomte"? The user account in question offers no clues of any kind. If for the sake of obfuscation, to cause seven years of bickering, then Lecomte (presumably) has found great success. It is dismissed as amateurish avant-garde pap by so many, but a resilient number of fans find the film to be utterly disregarding of labels. It only wants to infect the way one thinks about horror movies. Or, some have suggested, it simply wants to infect the way one thinks.

Lecomte's role in the film's production is unclear, really. It is not known when he is present, when he is manning the camera, and when he is "off set." It's possible that Lecomte shot the entire film himself, and the other three are seen just often enough to support this assumption, though several scenes of "imminent peril" clash with others in which Lecomte (again, presumably, because he is never seen) is eerily calm. Few of the shots have the almost prerequisite found-footage tremor. Whoever held that camera was a stout-hearted fellow. The one indication that Lecomte had any involvement other than as an avatar uploading the file is simply that "Bald" looks at the camera before they go down to the cellar and mumbles, "Whatever. It's your deal, Lecomte."

So through the mire of questions, the October Film Haunt intends to find the house and go under it. There are a couple of vague boasts in message boards—such as that of a small ghost-hunting group based in Vermont, now defunct, judging from their website—that claim the house has been found, but to the best of the online world's knowledge, no one has ever confirmed this. But we believe we've spotted a clue, so the game's afoot...

Mayne

Once they knew where the house was, the thought of going ate at them. Cheung would joke that they should change the name to the August Film Haunt, then the September Film Haunt. But tradition held them. They took a road trip once a year and camped out at the location or basis of a famous horror film, preferably one with some dark rumor attached, and this year the choice was unanimous.

Cheung had figured out where it was using an obscured, rotted sign he'd spotted nailed to a tree near the end of the film. Neither Mayne nor Harlan had ever noticed it before, and only after Cheung sharpened the image a few times on his computer did the sign look like it might read CORD LAKE, and a couple of weeks later he had the house, the lake and the woods, deep in northern New Hampshire, pulled up on Google Earth.

As writers, their goal was inspiration, vibe absorption. They'd never used cameras (until this trip, though Cheung's handheld was still in its case) because they didn't like to rely on the visual of film. The power of words! Cheung came up with the chain story idea in 2011, at the mausoleum purported to be where the weird coda of the original *Blood in Your Things* was shot. A dry, prosaic aura had greeted them there, but the story they'd cobbled together hadn't been half bad. One or two thousand words each, third-person POV, past tense for the appropriate detachment, then pass it on to the next writer. Fresh perspectives. The three of them got hooked on the format. Afterward, each was allowed to take his chunk of the story and mine it for other work, but the past two years they'd published as one on the October Film Haunt blog. The fictionalized journalism angle had a good audience with fellow movie geeks.

The key was to stick to the proscribed POV. To think of it as the guy who just won't let go of the camera even when the world is crumbling around him or zombies are lurking nearby. Thus Harlan vanished some other time, and all of this happened to some other person with his name. Mayne was keeping the third-person/past intact even though he realized he was going meta, breaking out of the construct through the description of the process. But he was sticking with it because he found himself jumping at every shadow, sitting in an upstairs bedroom of this fucked-up house, Cheung and Alem sleeping, or pretending to, against the opposite wall. Baily had left the room several minutes ago to explore the house, and Mayne had been too nervous to call her back.

Harlan's disappearance hadn't been as skin-crawling as Humley's. When Mayne joined the others, leading a hobbling Foster, still looking years older and hollowed out, by the collar, Harlan jumped to his feet, dropped the journal in the ashes of the old fire, and announced he had to piss. He stared at the border collie for a long moment before walking toward the trees, away from the house to the west. Mayne leaned forward and checked Foster's mouth to be sure, but they could already see the wooden crown wasn't there. Instead he found two pale wooden splinters on the dog's tongue.

In the film, after Humley runs into the trees and the campfire spreads into a perfect ring of flames, after the men blur and elongate beyond the screen, the rest of the crew can be seen in the distance, going back into the house. Mayne, Cheung, and Alem went back, too, but only after they had the good grace to shout Harlan's name for half an hour into the dark. When the cold drove them inside, they stood at the staircase, a naked thing with its banister torn away, and looked around. Baily filled the entire house with a long, undulating howl. That decided them, and up they went.

Mayne had an idea where Harlan might be. They all did. The thought of it made his stomach hurt, even with the horror-movie hope that Harlan was playing a doozy of a practical joke on them.

So far everything had been the four of them deliberately following the sequence of the film, observing, tapping into something that hadn't been present at the three other film haunts Mayne had been a part of. The wooden crown had yet to turn up. Mayne was thankful—of all the movies and art pieces he'd watched in his life, all the books, it was the one thing that had ever given him nightmares. The thought of it pulled and pushed in his head. But perhaps more importantly, and more immediate, there had been no faces at the window. He sat on top of his sleeping bag, the Coleman lantern hissing beside him, and tried not to look at that window, keeping it in the corner of his eye.

"As long as there's no crown," he whispered.

Foster, however, sat staring right at the window. Mayne had only known the dog for three weeks, but it wasn't the same Foster that had jumped into Alem's Jetta wagon three days ago and started licking Baily's mouth. That Foster had been three years old but thought he was still a puppy. Now he seemed elderly, full of a calm and weary resignation. Catatonic, or close to it, not answering to his name or anything else, no matter how Mayne pitched his voice or scratched the magic spot on Foster's rump. He just stared at the window, waiting for faces that hadn't looked in yet.

"Was it something in that grass, boy?" Mayne put his hand on the dog's back, then leaned over and buried his face in the thick black fur. It smelled like the forest. He wrapped him in his arms and squeezed. "If I give you your own name," he said, "will you come back?"

A rope of drool reached from Foster's jaw to the floor. It pooled there.

"I'll call you Moon. Your breed does best with kids, families. That's what I was going to find for you. But you'll stay with me, and every night I can say 'Goodnight, Moon.' Yeah? Sound okay, boy? Is that a silly name?"

The dog could have been carved out of wood.

Cheung

The silence of the house seemed to have layers. Cheung woke from his half-sleep and sat up, listening. Beneath Mayne's crying and wet sniffling, as he tried to bring his dog back from whatever piece of the ether he'd gone to. Beneath Alem's soft, girlish snores. Cheung felt as though the house had slowly inhaled before their arrival and had been on the verge of whispering to him ever since.

He hardly cared about the film haunt anymore. The blog and the novel he'd never started. He felt that Lecomte was here in this house. Perhaps under it, yes, or even *of* the house. It wouldn't be the first time that trope had raised its head. But there was almost a smell in the air, a taste. The house was full of *almost*s and a familiar dread he'd never known before.

Baily had left the room. He almost got up to go look for her. He knew he should, but his bones were too heavy. That other half of sleep came upon him now. For a moment something seemed to peer at him from just beyond the doorway, but it was nothing. He settled back into his sleeping bag.

[a word or name here has been scratched out with heavy strokes]

Lecomte

I learned what they call themselves this time. I wanted to help the telling.

"Cheung" and "Alem" woke to "Mayne" crashing to the floor, shrieking, kicking himself backward across the floor.

"What? What is it?" Alem struggled his way out of his sleeping bag.

Mayne pointed at the window, pointed again, his hand stabbing at the air. "Faces! Looking in. From the video!"

The window, all twelve panes of it, was empty. Cheung went to Mayne, tried to lift him to his feet. "Calm down, man. There's nothing there."

Foster hobbled over to the far corner of the room. The hot tang of urine filled the room and the dog collapsed onto the puddle. Cheung went to the window and looked up, saw an arm, splayed fingers, disappearing over the edge of the roof. Or, not disappearing, but being slowly withdrawn now that it had been seen. He looked down and there was "Harlan," pacing back and forth by the tree line, holding something pressed to his chest, obscured in the dark.

Alem came up beside him. "Do you see any—it's Harlan!"

But Cheung didn't hear him. His forehead pressed against the cold glass as he studied what Harlan was carrying. "He's got Baily. What the fuck is he doing with her?"

Harlan looked up at them, stood frozen for a moment, then dropped the dog to the ground. She didn't move. She looked rumpled, somehow, like a pile of laundry. Cheung smacked a palm against the window, turned to leave the room. Alem caught his arm and pulled him back. "Look."

I watched them from the doorway. Below, through other eyes, I saw Harlan wrap his arms around the trunk of a spruce and scurry up into its branches, spider-quick. Mayne had now joined them at the window. "We need to leave," he said, his words panicked and short of breath, "I'm not staying here, guys. We have to go now, go call the police, something."

He went on like that, devolving into a stream of nonsense, but Cheung just stared down at the lump of yellow that was Baily. Waiting for her to move.

When she didn't, they left the room, not seeing what had withdrawn into the greater shadows of the hallway. Downstairs and outside together, their lungs hitching in our northern chill. Between their leaving the window and rounding the corner of the house, the dog had either been removed or revived. She was gone from them.

Alem looked up into the tree Harlan had climbed. Cheung knelt and traced his fingers around where Baily had lain. Their tips were smeared with blood.

The three of them shouted for Harlan. Cheung soon stopped and shouted for Baily instead. The top of the tree shook, twenty feet or so off the ground, but neither the man nor the dog returned to them.

"This is. This is..." Alem didn't know what to say. He clearly wanted to get to his car and leave, but that meant forty-five minutes through the darkness of the trees. All the light they had brought with them, and no comfort to go with it.

"This is messed up, is what it is," Mayne said. "You do realize that one of us has just climbed a tree in the middle of the night." His voice was wavering again, hitting panic notes.

Perhaps the other two imagined their mates, keeping their beds warm far away in their homes. Surely they sifted through what they remembered of the final minutes of *Under the House*, down in the cellar.

But Cheung said, "We're staying and we're going under this house." He looked at each of them. "Why? Because Harlan *does* happen to be our friend, in case you've forgotten.

And there's something real here. You guys feel it. The film is real. We're getting something amazing out of this shit."

"That's exactly why I want to leave, man," Alem said, and the conversation dried up there, as if this were all nothing but their small talk.

They shouted up at Harlan some more, but the branches stilled and the night grew quiet again. Finally something came crashing down toward them, striking Alem's shoulder and rolling away into the wild grass. He went over and nudged the crown with his foot. In the film it is a beautiful jaundiced orange in the firelight, but here under the moon it breathed with a subtler, regal silver. It was made from wood, taken from any one of these trees, rough-hewn, unfinished and thin. Alem imagined his fingertips against the rough grain, tracing the three long tapers that rose over the head of the wearer. His scalp began to itch and tighten, loosen, tighten again.

He reached down from a great height, his hand at the last instant knocked aside by Mayne's boot, which stomped on the crown in a dry splitting snap. Our eyes closed against the sound, and I sighed with loss. Alem had fallen onto his side and was looking up into Mayne's face. "Hell, no, not that thing," the latter said, panting, shaking his head side to side. "No way, man."

Alem turned his head away in a sudden, bitter disappointment, and saw the window above filling up. Two figures stood looking down at them from the same bedroom they had minutes ago vacated. The window glass was warped from this angle, or else the two peering faces were smudged into dark blurs. I smiled up at these faces. I smiled out at my new friends, but still they did not see. So I left them, to return their book to its place.

Harlan

Morning. The others said to write my part, about what I

did. They don't see someone else has been writing, too. Light is gray, coming strained by the woods through the window in bars on the scarred floorboards. Dust in the light. On the wall the black dog's skin hangs on a hook. It sags like a coat and I giggle. The blood on the floor beneath it has already dried. I don't think the others even noticed when they rose. They only asked where I had been and I did not answer.

Came out of the tree in the night. Back to the house and slept next to Mayne until the dog's skin came off. Pen sticks to the sap on my hand, smeared all red. Sap runs thick this time of year. All night, figures standing in our doorway without faces.

I'm supposed to say for someone's father: here in New Hampshire is a pretty place, forests and old homes the trees took. The others don't know I'm supposed to. Thetford. Thetford is the place. So look for the sign in the forest.

Pictures in my head won't come out for the paper. Close my eyes and see I have shrunk to a very small point and the walls are paper tunnels and dripping slow honey. There is a light impossible enough to hold everything inside it. We must crawl to it. The way we get there is through the honeyed tunnels. Into eyes that yawn open into mouths. After, I think the mouths might go on to the stars and the black they hold between them, until all we know about our world and every world and all our thoughts are just a blood clot in something's veins.

I open my eyes to go under the house. The others are speaking down at the bottom of the stairs, but all I hear is a hum. I stop writing now. These pictures stay in my head. I will have to show them.

Alem

Alem took the film haunt journal from Harlan and started to flip back to skim his entry, so he'd know where to pick up.

But there was something in Harlan's eyes, an indistinctness to his face, and for the briefest instant he could have sworn Harlan was wearing the crown, his head tilted nearly onto his shoulder. Instead he turned to a blank page and recorded his entry, with difficulty willing himself not to write, *This feels like the part where we're all going to die here.* And of course he realized he'd written it anyway.

Cheung still hadn't mentioned Baily to Harlan, but it was there on his face. In the air around them, any minute now. That one of them could kill a dog and spend half the night up a tree and not have any questions to answer the next morning—it spoke volumes of how freaked out everyone was.

"Okay, we can leave now," Alem said, giving up on pretense. Everything he said now approached a higher octave, and he paced a tight oval in the foyer, between the staircase and the front door, still writing in the journal. He remembered something Mayne had told him during the long drive up: You are the cameraman who won't put the damned thing down when everything is going to hell around you.

"Foster's dead, isn't he?" Mayne said. It felt like he was asking the empty, dim house as much as his three friends. "Isn't he?"

"I'm not leaving until I find Baily," Cheung said, and the thin wall of tension broke. He shoved Harlan against a wall, close to shouting down into his face. "What did you do with her?"

Harlan looked away and smiled. The smile belonged on the face of a child, knowing and wistful and cold. Knowing, for a moment later they all heard a scratching from the rear of the house, nails on wood, and a pitiful whimper.

"Foster?" Mayne called down the short hallway.

"Foster's a coat hanging from a hook," Harlan sputtered, still smiling, still pressed against the wall by Cheung's forearm on his neck. "Didn't you see? You never see."

"No, that's Baily," Cheung said, leaning in close to Harlan's face. "You put her in the basement, asshole, great." And he let him go. Harlan slumped to the floor, coughing and rubbing his neck.

"Cheung, come on," Mayne said. "Let her up and let's go."

A yelp and a sound of something falling down stairs. Cheung ran toward the kitchen. Harlan crawled over to Cheung's bag and pulled the small blocky camera out. He grinned up at the others. "For pictures."

"A thousand words," Mayne said. The pen snapped in Alem's hand then, cutting his palm just below the index finger. Ink bled onto the paper and sought the crevice between pages. He held onto the stub of pen, scratched out the remaining words, as if they were his last.

**"Under *Under the House*," by Charles Mayne
Posted on www.filmhaunt.com, September 2015**

Following the several minutes of acid trip imagery that come after the fire and the crown—bizarre video flaws such as doubling and reshaping; a figure wearing the dog's skin climbing on top of a sleeping man; eighty leisurely, jarringly sunny seconds of first-person POV passing through the woods as the lake glitters through branches ahead; things crawling along the walls outside the house—the film abruptly rights itself, relatively speaking, and the morning begins with a linear calm. The crew members gather at the basement door, the camera pointed at the floor and three sets of legs. After a few moments you realize you have noted the red Nikes the bald man is wearing. The bald man speaks to Lecomte in resignation, and the four of them descend the stairs.

And with all the speculation and picking-apart of *Under*

the House's ending, its dread and tension and Lynchian obliqueness, more than anything else it's that sound that haunts us. What is it? Was it added to the footage later? It's an easy thing to hope not. There's so much about the film that feels authentic, one expects its creepiness to remain well earned. There are still a few dozen YouTube videos out there, from half-attempts at speculation to parodies in which the figures coming down the stairs after the crew members are revealed to be bright-colored clowns with party favors in their mouths. Or, as is the case with several from 2010, soccer players blowing plastic vuvuzela horns.

At first it is only a cellar, earthen and surprisingly small. In the weak yellow light of the camera, an irregular hole appears in the far wall, at floor level, with a large stone disc propped beside it. The hole is initially in the frame only in passing, yet is palpably clear as the destination. Because surely naming the film *Under the House* does not refer to this nondescript square cellar with nothing more than a dirt floor and pale brick walls.

"There were other things here before," Humley says. He seems shaken and nervy. No one answers him, and the viewer is left to assume they have come down here at some other, undocumented time.

The door opens above them with a faint creak. The camera turns to the stairs as the sound begins. Though others disagree, as though the nature of the sound depends on its hearer, I can only describe it as a great hum run backward through a tape deck, littered with clicks and dirty filters, but somehow more wet-sounding. Folded inside the world. The swelling chant of a beehive, breathed deep in a forgotten room through cheap speakers. And at the same time nothing like these things.

The tread of feet on the stairs, then the shoes themselves—brown boots, bare feet, black sneakers, and those vivid red shoes with the white Nike swooshes. Then the legs descend into the frame, and the hum grows fuller and more distorted. There's a burst of moaning, movement. The camera rushes across the cellar and dips down shaking into that black hole. The film goes on in that blackness for more than a minute before the video cuts off, but you know it has already ended because the hum is gone.

Only the one question remains.

Camera

The screen is gray and striped with shivering bands as it descends the staircase into dimness and sweeps around to show the close cellar. Cheung is visible by the near wall, crouched over something. Yellow whiteness flares in the bottom left corner and the cellar comes into sharper relief.

"Cheung?" Mayne's voice says, off-camera. "She okay?"

Alem moves into the frame holding a lantern. His other hand reaches out and touches Cheung, who stands up and walks toward the center of the dirt floor. The camera lingers on the dog for several seconds. She is not okay. Only by moving the camera closer is it apparent that Baily is still breathing, in shallow pulses along her ribcage, the fur matted red. Her eyes are rolled up to the whites.

"The other one's a coat," Harlan says, and the screen moves with the rhythm of his laughter.

"There's the hole," someone says, and the view shifts to show the cavity in the brick wall, a thick slab of stone leaning beside it. At this point the audio flattens and is swallowed by a new sound. A shrieking low hum, as if many rusted doors are slowly opening, that is felt in the fabric of the video.

"Jesus God," a voice shouts. The camera, which begun to move toward the hole, turns again. Four figures are coming down the stairs, and as Mayne, Cheung, and Alem run toward and then past Harlan, the figures reach the cellar floor. The lantern has been left at the foot of the stairs, and in its wash of light four blurred smudges look across at the screen. Slowly, as though the lens is correcting its focus, the smudges diminish to reveal Mayne, Cheung, Alem, and Harlan, the head of each tilted far toward the left shoulder. Their mouths are open, emitting or inhaling the deep squelching sound.

Harlan—the one holding the camera—giggles and says, "Hi."

The four men don't respond. The new Alem knocks the lantern over, gently, and the cellar clicks into darkness.

"The way we get there is through the tunnels," the first Harlan says. Something is muttered, a shuffle and scrape close to the microphone. The camera comes alive with night vision, Harlan's shoes glowing with an alien green. He laughs again as the screen lifts to show the four doppelgängers moving rapidly toward Harlan. "Okay, the pictures are in here!" He turns and scrambles into the hole in the wall, green phosphorescence trailing back like blacklit algae in the sudden movement.

The screen rolls and tumbles for a moment, then straightens itself. The sound of stone grinding on stone is heard, as perhaps the disc is rolled over the hole in the cellar above. A large chamber spreads out on the screen, fuzzy and fluorescent in the night vision, its walls expanding away from the camera. The impression is something of a resuscitated lung filling with air. Beneath Harlan's feet the surface of the floor sinks and flexes, suggesting some form of organic material.

It is difficult to ascertain this new environment. Vaguely spheroid, the chamber resembles both a honeycomb and a catacomb. There are wet sounds and noises of things sliding. The camera moves forward and stumbles to the floor. Harlan's leg has sunk into a hole that stretches perhaps four feet across. It is one of dozens, perhaps hundreds, of holes that line the chamber. He lifts the leg and his bare foot brings ropes of thick liquid with it. "Probably looks green to you, huh?" he says. "It's kind of orange, really. Like a golden orange in the morning. I think it's honey, just like I wrote before."

The camera moves with caution now and pans across the sides of the chamber. Many of the holes, or slots, are occupied. A face peers out of one on the right side, openmouthed and covered in what looks like mint jelly. The camera makes its way to him. Mayne is struggling weakly, and after a moment it's clear he is trying to turn himself around in the shaft.

"You don't look so good, Mr. Charlie Mayne." Harlan's voice is full of a trembling excitement. "You ready to see the pictures? You ready to go into the mouth? It goes far and maybe all the way to forever. Alem!" Harlan tracks to the left and finds another figure, which is also turning itself feet first to crawl into the tunnel. "There's..." Harlan pauses, scanning across the chamber, revealing several faces peeping out of holes along the wall. "There's a lot of people here. There's Longhair from the movie! Can I have your autograph?" A fit of wild giggles ends in wet coughing.

On the screen, a bald man and a man with long ropes of green-gleaming hair can be seen craning their necks, sniffing at the air, then withdrawing into privacy. Dozens of other figures, several women among them, do the same. Many extend their bodies out of the holes to the waist, exposing elongated torsos and arms, before retracting them.

"Cheung! Hey, Cheung!" Harlan yells. "I'm looking for Cheung, guys. Wait, there's those famous long legs, Yao Ming! See his shoes over there?" Harlan's arm reaches into the frame and points. "Never mind. He's gone now. I want to see, too."

The camera falls to the floor, and threaded with a shimmering green, Harlan is seen hoisting himself up into a vacant hole. He pauses to smear a substance over his face, looks down at the camera with a grin, and crawls forward. A great moist thrum fills the chamber, unlike the sound in the cellar above, heavier and with more motion. A ripple runs through the chamber wall, a powerful slow furrow, and the screen displays more than an hour of the mouth of Harlan's tunnel, until the camera is picked up and the screen goes black.

There is a pinkish blur of light. A face stares down into the screen, then a hand appears and covers the lens. A room appears in murky daylight when the hand is removed a moment later, and the face is clearer. Its skin is a grayish orange, hairless. Its eyes extend the width of the face and around the temples. The nose and mouth are not visible.

The figure sets the camera down on a table, facing a large gray laptop computer and an empty chair. It is a dining room, with no curtains over the two windows in frame. The figure sits in the chair and connects a thin cable to the computer, then reaches toward the camera with the cord's other end. The screen shifts an inch or so then steadies. The figure opens a thick leatherbound book and drapes one strangely long arm across the table, so that its hand can write.

Two minutes and fourteen seconds into this writing, the figure pauses and looks up, beyond the camera. It smiles, and its mouth appears when it does so, along what would have been considered its jawline a moment before. The room brightens rapidly, as though the entire house is filling with light. It is a white light, blooming and pushing rather than merely intensifying, and is followed by a deep tremble and groaning. Plaster sifts in curtains, dusting the seated figure with more white, and the camera fills with flickering digital snow. The long eyes squeeze closed, perhaps in the savoring of something, and the video is lost in light.

Lecomte

Oh, these eyes. All my Father's eyes.

He is hungry for coming stars. Strings of them like pearls in His belly. Ever since He fell from the stars and we planted Him in the earth to grow. To find out what He would be in His bloom. I sit and I finish the book the children brought, and find pleasure in my film bringing interest into their lives. The lives of many others. But Father is so nearly ripe now, to His brim. It cannot be long for our emergence into open air.

I shall sign my name, here, and I shall send some final lovely images to satisfy all their curiosities. If Father is not full, He will wait for this larger meal. And all the old stars will come back for Him with all the old black strung between them.

Bring me my Father's eyes, children.

Oh, but this movement and this light. This light that comes from Father's mouth! Is He now?

—M. Lecomte

Deducted From Your
Share in Paradise

The women fell from the sky, silhouetted as dying eagles against the sunset. They struck the huddled trailers of Twin Firs and buckled thin ceilings, the sound of their impacts like God drumming His fingers briefly on the earth. Inside the trailers, residents shrank to the floors, then grew curious and swiped grimed windows to watch the end of this quick strange rain. The land was packed tight as stone and some of the women broke upon it, but others answered its shock and lay somehow blinking at the fading day.

Quiet yawned in the wake. Fen watched the scrims of dust settle from his vantage in Acre Field and had to hold Murray close against his leg lest the coonhound lope back toward home. He searched the emptied sky, its expanse bruising blue-black as the horizon lifted to take the last of the sun. "That couldn't have been people," Fen said, even though he'd marked the flutter of cloth and spread arms reaching up toward the first stars. Nothing like the shapes of great birds.

Murray barked once, a deep chuff low in his chest. Fen

tightened his fingers around the collar and listened to the silent ripple still spreading across the unyielding ground. He stood not three hundred feet from the nearest trailer but for a long moment he felt in another county.

"Come on, boy," he said at last. It was necessary to hunch over as he walked the dog across the faded ribbon of road. "You behave. Why, they could be angels for all we know, falling like that." They passed through knee-high grass and down a grade into the trailer park's shallow bowl.

The first woman lay sprawled just inside the loose ring of single-wides. Pieces of the wooden sign reading Twin Firs jutted from beneath her like jetsam. Her dress was of creased black linen and rendered her complexion a creamy white against it. She could have just come from a funeral in heaven, though she had no wings or even a single feather upon her person. Her hair was a dull brown and her lips moved rhythmically as one who chants a prayer under her breath. She stared up at the fresh night where the tips of stars began to pierce the curtains. An owl flung itself from a tree and picked a bat from the air near the nimbus of the lone streetlamp.

"Miss, you all right?" Fen lowered onto one knee and laid a hand on the woman's sleeve. It was hot to the touch and he imagined the air baking around her flesh. Still he shook her arm. Still her wide black eyes fixed upon the firmament and her mouth made soundless entreaties toward it.

"Hush, Murray," he said when the hound tipped his head to howl. He stood and walked around her, to the center of the park. His eyes picked out more women draped in black dresses, nearly all gazing up as though condemned and full of broken, numbed bones. Most were strewn about the weedy lot. One had smashed the hood of Daddy Pardon's Buick. Our only running car, Fen almost said aloud. Another dangled from his own bowed roof, a brown arm close to brushing the top of the trailer's door. The inverted face regarded Fen and murmured a litany.

Fen kept his grip on Murray's collar and waited for the women to move or for the trailer doors to open. Faces peered out of windows until at last one brave soul stepped out. The exodus followed.

"What is it, Fen?" Sterla called across. Her hair was wet and the shroud of her nightgown didn't cover nearly enough of her. Each of her twin boys steadied her with a hand upon her shoulder.

Hawk came out from the next trailer and spat from between greasy curtains of hair. "Looks like a bunch of ladies just fell out of the sky, Sterla."

"Guess the drought's done," Daddy Pardon said, and grinned for a cold moment. His thumbs were tucked into his belt like a caricature of a lawman. "Peculiar way to end it. Come on, let's get these girls up and see they ain't hurt."

"Hurt?" Sterla said. "They should every one be dead." At Daddy Pardon's sharp glance her face clouded with an impertinent blush.

Fen counted eleven of the women while the others conferred. None was exactly beautiful but each carried a sort of reposed grace. Several were the color of snow, which Fen had never seen, and some were darker than the tree trunks painted on the ruined sign. Three, though, lay facedown and arranged in unnatural angles. Fen rolled these last over and clamped a hand over his mouth. Their faces were cracked like china and along the cracks ran seams of drying blood. The whites of the eyes had crusted black.

He stood and saw the preacher's eyes glitter from the folded shadows between two trailers. A tall column of paler dark and the rim of his felt hat catching nearby window light.

The preacher watched from his recess as the ambassadors of the occupied trailers gathered in the lot. Old Grady leaned on his cane wheezing his disbelief. Fen thought that perhaps the fallen women had been waiting for the full turnout, for once Reed Jens shuffled up shirtless and gripping his whiskey bottle, the eight survivors sat up in unison and turned their heads to take in the small crowd. They held their arms out in supplication, like dolls.

Sterla fainted, the sound a softer thunderclap than the women had made but no less heavy there in the dust.

•

Daddy Pardon took three of the women for himself. The other trailers were allotted one visitor save the preacher, who never left his wedge of dark as the women clasped the hands of the residents. The preacher repaired to his trailer and his Bible. When his earthy baritone soon moistened the night outside the windows, not one among the congregation attended the sundown sermon, delivered daily under the stars from a warped bookshelf that doubled as his pulpit.

Fen listened to the lonesome hymns. The girl Daddy Pardon had given him sat in his living room partition on the sprung couch. Her hands folded loosely upon her lap and her great and dark eyes divided their attention between the ceiling and her host. Her hair was a rust orange parted cleanly in the middle. He guessed this was the youngest of them, close to his own years, as among them only she still seemed at the end of blossoming. Murray lay with his head on his forepaws. He stared at the girl with reddened eyes and issued an occasional huffing sigh that fluttered his chops. Fen took this as a hesitant approval.

She mouthed her silent flow of words at his questions. Fen abandoned conversation and boiled a package of hot dogs on the stove. He folded each in a slice of white bread. He slathered mustard across one and when he handed it to the girl she sniffed it, then sucked the mustard off and laid the rest on her dress.

"Go on, you should eat," he told her. He lifted the bread onto a plate and squeezed more mustard along the meat and returned it to her. Again she held the food to her nose before licking it clean.

"Well. All right, then," Fen said and gave two of the dogs to Murray. He wondered what to do next. He asked her again where they came from and how come most weren't hurt when they landed and why here in Twin Firs. The girl would only answer with the moving lips and unwavering, empty gaze.

Outside the singing stopped and the preacher began to moan scripture in a liquid voice. Fen looked out the window and saw the bodies of the three dead women as black lumps in the dirt lot. He pulled the curtains shut and exaggerated his yawn. Behind him the girl echoed the gesture with a mouthful of strange teeth.

*

The town of El Hueco lay dying around them and not one in their trailer park tilled any soil or punched any time clock. Daddy Pardon carried the self-appointed governor's yoke around his neck and meted out the residents' pocket money. He collected the government checks that arrived in the letterboxes once a month, which sufficed to cover the gas and electric and the weekly harvest at the Citgo two miles up County Road 6. If folks needed new pants or shoes, it was Daddy Pardon's onus to inspect the old ones for holes.

Fen steered as clear of that man as he could, which on their two acres of cracked earth was hardly at all. His father had been sent away when the boy was eleven. All Fen had left of him was the coffee can buried in the dirt beneath the trailer. The can held a stained family photograph and a roll of nearly five hundred dollars sealed in a baggie. Fen's mother had been dead three years and still he waited for Daddy Pardon to knock on his door with a shovel.

The next morning found the sullen vista of Twin Firs altered. It now featured the fallen women on the flat roofs peeling strips of metal and hammering at the damage their bodies had done. Others scrubbed the filth from trailer walls, rags and sponges floating in buckets of soapy water, or plucked weeds from the lot and carted bags of trash to the row of bins by the road. Daddy Pardon directed them, a cigarette clamped in his mouth and its smoke crawling over the brim of his ten-gallon hat.

Fen had watched them drag away the bodies of their dead kin before they settled into their chores. Already the corpses crumbled into ash. His eyes rarely left his own guest. She was smaller than the others but just as steadfast. He realized she needed a name if she had none she would share.

The other residents observed the women with a tired wonder. By half past nine the day was sealed in a heavy envelope of heat. Sterla sat on a sagging lawn chair and fanned herself with the lid of a Styrofoam cooler. Her sons sprayed the women with a hose that had sprung several leaks like twigs on a branch. Fen suspected they enjoyed the look of the wet linen clinging to the women's curves. The women paid no mind but toiled without pause under the ferocious sun. If Fen squinted he could see their mouths moving, always moving in their silence.

"If they're angels," Sterla said late that morning, "then where's their wings? Why ain't they said a word?"

"Might be they have to earn back their wings," Daddy Pardon said. He reached down a pink hand and squeezed himself between the legs. "Might be we can get 'em talking some." Fen turned away and took Murray back into their trailer to wait out the sun.

The second evening the preacher again found himself without a flock. His pastorship had come unmoored and he sang and reveled in one last empty sunset without harmony. He would worship in private beginning the next day.

Fen opened his door one noon to see the preacher wearing a smile that did not touch the small pebbles of his eyes beneath the hat brim. The time-softened Bible lay against the man's breast. Short taps and squeals of metal came from above as Fen's girl worked on the roof. The A/C unit struggled, rattling against the window frame.

The preacher stepped up into the trailer. "God has sent us each a trial, young man," he said, his eyes turned to heaven and the girl between him and that place. The familiar sundown inflection entered his voice, rising and falling on swells of spirit. "Those women were cast out and you embrace what He saw fit for Hell."

Fen regarded his shoes. "They don't seem like that, preacher," he said.

"We must likewise cast them out, son. Every glance upon them is a sin. Each invitation to our homes, each nail they send into that roof—" he pointed with a long raisin-skinned finger "—is likened unto a nail driven into Christ, and what are we but His body?"

Fen felt muddled with confusion. The preacher often had this effect on him. One day they were the exalted flesh of the Lord God and the next no more than the thirsty dust trodden beneath His feet.

"Each moment you give them," the preacher said, "will be deducted from your share in Paradise."

With this he retreated into the heat. Fen watched him rap on Daddy Pardon's door. Somehow the girl had gotten back into Fen's trailer. She whispered unknowable words to his back and he turned around and smiled at her.

•

He named her Gloria. It was a name made for an angel,

if angel she was. He used it in everything he said to her in hopes she would come to claim it. With the name he learned to taste the flavor of her various silences. She still did not speak—none of the women did—and he settled on an attempt to teach her wordless gestures.

He received his first smile five days after she and the others fell out of the sky. She caught him staring as she gazed at the ceiling and the corners of her thin red mouth curled up, stiffly, as if those muscles had never been used before.

That evening he gave her his bed and slept on the carpet next to Murray. It offered more comfort than the sunken couch. The floor thinned his sleep and he woke once when the hound kicked his legs within gentle nightmares. Gloria sat on his bunk watching him and practicing her smile, her eyes black hollows in the dark.

Two nights later he joined her and they lay entwined in their clothes on the narrow mattress. Gloria murmured her unending litanies as Fen reached his hand to the hem of her dress. He did this in a relentless fashion but drew back each time. His fingers felt as though they would soil her. The preacher's words hung like gnats in the air.

He settled for the touch of her exposed skin, savored it, and listened to the trailer park's night sounds. Twin Firs had always been a quiet place in spite of its thin walls. It remained so now but there were layers he could hear beneath the hush and the ambient shake of the air conditioner. From the right Fen caught a lilt to Old Grady's moans that spoke of something far from pain. Hawk's trailer creaked across the way in a steady rhythm. Fen pictured it trembling in its frame but did not untangle himself from Gloria to go to the window.

The noises he least wanted to hear issued from Sterla's trailer. Keening gasps like steam from a kettle and "Oh Mama" caught in a loop that followed him into sleep.

•

Gloria was always gone when he awoke in the mornings, her smell of old books lingering in the sheets. He put her in the shower once, averting his eyes until she understood the water's purpose and could bathe herself, and was somehow comforted when the scent stayed upon her.

Outside the women had begun to tear apart the twenty-odd vacant trailers and amass a heap of wood joists and aluminum panels in the lot. Fen took to sitting on his cinderblock steps and watching Gloria as she and her folk assembled what looked to be a large shed. They were uncanny with carpentry. The structure grew quickly from the ground and each new portion was painted a vivid red before they moved to the next. Fen couldn't figure out where they got the red paint from. No one had been to town.

Of the residents, only Daddy Pardon and the preacher emerged from their homes. The former seemed to lose his clothes along the way, stepping into the sun each afternoon nearer to nakedness as he shook the trailer doors to no avail. He peered through windows and shouted. The residents were required to tender their government checks in person at the EZ Cash in town before Daddy Pardon could pad the treasury. Angry rashes crept from his yellowed underwear and the skin of his back between the shoulders, the blades of which swelled as though with tumors.

The preacher beseeched the locked doors with less violence. He sermonized in the dust before Fen and the hound, casting the trailer park as a modern Babel, the unknown structure red as Satan.

Fen did see Hawk once, standing slumped beside his trailer one morning, an unfocused glaze to his eyes. "You liking yours?" he asked Fen.

The boy blushed and made a noncommittal noise.

"Never tasted such sweetness between a woman's legs," Hawk said, his tongue reaching out to lick slow across the upper lip. "It's like heaven. I reckon that does make them

111

angels."

"How do you know they want that, if they can't talk? Seems they'd just want to get back home." Fen looked up into Hawk's weathered face. Sterla called him Mexican but Old Grady said he was an Injun. Hawk never corrected either, choosing to let both labels stick.

"What else would they be for, smelling like they do? Tasting like that? They didn't fall from heaven to play Scrabble and watch the soaps." Hawk smiled and shuffled back inside. The back of his t-shirt bulged, like a rag was wadded below its neck.

Whatever desire lay in their silence, each sundown brought the women back to their appointed hosts. Fen and Gloria lay in their chaste bed amidst the intruding sounds of strange ecstasy throughout Twin Firs. Her skin remained dry as brittle paper. Fen came to know that he loved her but still denied his body the confession of it. He tried to guess how far north five hundred dollars would get them and Murray. He'd never been more than an hour's walk from the trailer park. Mexico simmered only forty miles below but he longed to see snow and firs that weren't painted on a broken sign. Not more scrubland. He felt the girl's breath against his neck and wondered if she would follow.

•

It was three more days before Fen asked her. When he could get her away from her kin and their tireless work, the two of them took walks around the trailer park, through Acre Field up onto the short lip of earth that looked over what might have been a lake in some era ancient to Fen. It was all hardpan now, unused and unseen. He was able to more clearly regret the surroundings in which he'd lived his small life, and to wish there were something green and thriving he could share with her. Even so, Gloria smiled often now, and several times he caught a blush in her cheeks as she glanced at the ground.

Murray began brushing his side against her as they walked, rather than sticking to Fen's side like the glue he'd been since puppyhood. Every time Gloria reached down to scratch behind the hound's ears, Fen thought he could feel a hole inside himself that was changing into the shape of her.

At last, one evening back in the trailer, he stumbled through the words. "Would you want to go away with me and Murray?" He let a minute grind in the mill of his patience, clenching his jaw. The corners of her mouth, stained with mustard, twitched in her attempted smiles. He daubed her lips with a napkin, held her hands and got down on his knees.

"See, Daddy Pardon's why I lost my real dad," he said. "He run him off when I was a kid, said he'd been holding back money. Thing was, he *had* kept some, slow over the years. It was his, wasn't it? About the last thing he ever told me was he'd buried it for when I grew up. After that Daddy Pardon took my mama for his own. I think she died of shame."

Gloria began to nod as he'd taught her. Fen trembled from the telling of the story. He'd never breathed a word of it before unless he counted Murray.

"You'll do it? I already dug up the money can. You'll leave the others and come north?"

Gloria flapped her arms in a birdlike motion then laid her hands on Fen's shoulders, repeating the two gestures until Fen said, "You want us to fly away?" She nodded faster. For a moment Fen glimpsed the long inward curves of her teeth.

"But you don't have any wings," he said. She shook her head and patted his shoulders again, then pointed at him. Murray laid his muzzle across her knee and looked up at her. Fen didn't know if it was affection or the hot dog she held in her lap.

Gloria's eyes shone. He realized they were tears when one broke free and slipped down her cheek.

•

August filled the thermometer outside Fen's door with blood red. The trailers gave off a bloated smell and were it not for the continuance of night noises Fen would have feared that most everyone had died of heatstroke in those long coffins.

Daddy Pardon and the preacher had joined the others in reclusion and Fen alone surveyed the construction. Black symbols adorned the walls, sinuous and illegible shapes that made his vision swim. Beautiful curved lines. The women again looked insubstantial as birds, balanced with clinging ease as they ascended the new spire that had quickly grown from the squat building's roof upward to twenty feet, a lone and rumpled finger accusing the sky from which they had come.

On the sixth of August the residents emerged without preamble as the sun crawled into the west. Fen watched them from his cinderblock stoop. Sterla and her twins were the first. Then Hawk and Reed and Old Grady. The preacher was missing. They stood blank and worn and nude, gazing up at the women and the spreading colors of dusk. High on the back of each native was a rounded hump distending between the shoulder blades.

Daddy Pardon stormed from his trailer and shouted them into a line. "All of you got two checks now to cash," he said, his own sac of skin shifting on his back as he gestured wildly. Fen was the only resident there both clothed and without the odd disfigurement.

None moved or spoke or even looked at Daddy Pardon. Above them the noises of construction ceased and the women ranged across the building's roof, watching the scene. One by one they tossed their tools to the dirt below.

Their job was complete, or near enough. An alien thing hulking over the faded trailers with its tapered spire thrust in exclamation. The whole of it was doorless and hasty and Fen could not see the purpose it served.

"Fine then," Daddy Pardon said. "I'll see to it myself." He stalked off toward his subjects' homes, disappearing through Hawk's door.

Fen stared at the bulging sacs that stretched across the shoulder blades of those he had known from his childhood. Sterla in particular pained Fen's eyes, hunched as her girth was with the extra burden. But he did not restrain himself for further thought or a resolving glance toward Gloria. They needed more money.

His neighbors screened him as he moved toward Daddy Pardon's trailer. It was almost cool inside and the refrigerator door hung open. Fen rifled through cabinets and the chest of drawers before his eyes fell on the stained, sour-smelling bed. Under it he found a dented blue lockbox with more cash than he could guess at. He made a pouch of his t-shirt and crammed the bulk of the money into it.

Much too soon Daddy Pardon's voice was right outside the door. Fen scrambled onto the mattress and pushed the window out on its hinges and wormed through the tight gap, holding his shirt against his belly. The window frame caught him at the waist in a moment of panic. Fen hung there, scrabbling with his free hand as around the corner Daddy Pardon shouted that they were all worthless without him.

Fen tumbled to the ground just as the door banged open above him. He crawled to the rear before gaining his feet and running between two trailers. His heart bruised itself against his ribs as he leaned against a wall and jammed wads of money in his pockets. It was nearly dark. Low clouds bridged the horizons and it took Fen a moment to recognize them after the months of brutal open sky.

The preacher's face appeared glaring down at him from behind the dust-caked panes of his kitchen window. The barrel of a shotgun lay against his cheek and the smile on his face stilled Fen.

Until the women began to sing. It was perhaps language but carried a heavier import. A deep quavering harmony flooded through the park, and the sound of it was apocalyptic there in the hanging weariness of a land grown accustomed to their silence.

Murray's barks rounded the corner as the dog found his master. Fen buried his face in the speckled fur. From within his trailer Daddy Pardon's shriek and the crash of furniture wove into the women's chorus.

Fen and Murray crept around to view the transformation of the commune. Daddy Pardon waved the empty lockbox as he ran toward the residents, who were singing along with the visitors now and lifting their arms in a sort of reverence to the red temple. Mourning and hope converged within the notes and, as they slipped into a higher chord, Daddy Pardon's rage slipped away. He dropped the box and gave his weak tenor to the chorus.

In the center of the pall of clouds a blind eye opened and swirled. Several lightning bolts in succession reached down to grasp the tip of the red spire. The sky muttered an echo of each.

The first of the raindrops splashed Fen's face and he blinked. Gloria watched him from her perch and smiled as he moved closer and gestured her down. Her lips moved as ever but now the music issuing from them gave her new life and his heart deepened. A fresh and bitter stench filled the air as cold rain spattered the lot and raised chills on Fen's arms. More lightning raked the unhinging sky.

Old Grady fell to his knees with a grunt. The hump on his back lifted at each side, the skin ballooning. Sterla's twins followed with their hands scratching in the dirt as their own sacs strained outward. Fen stepped back. Soon the others were on all fours. Moans and gasps and above them the women singing the rain and the dark down.

A smaller thunder coughed and one of the women fell from the temple roof in a spray of red vibrant as the painted walls. She struck the ground, the front of her dress shredded and gaping. Fen turned to see the preacher breaking open his shotgun to rack a second shell.

"Pestilence!" the preacher screamed. He fired a blast into the sky. "Plague!"

Something dark erupted from Old Grady's shoulders as the rain became a hissing torrent percussing the earth. Fen stared as two great wings were born from the man's back, a rush of brown and black feathers, shaking themselves out to a span longer than the busted Buick.

The preacher raged to the heavens again and racked the shotgun. Behind Fen the women leapt to the ground.

Even as the sac on Daddy Pardon's back burst into a flexing shower of feathers, the big man lunged at Fen from his crouch, crying out for the money flowering from the boy's pockets.

A streak of black and Daddy Pardon was wrenched to the ground by Gloria. Her snarls had nothing of music in them. The preacher raised the gun toward her and Fen in turn tackled him, the gun discharging into the new mud.

In their loose semicircle the other residents sprouted the same powerful wings, and a woman climbed onto each of their backs. The dog howled as Fen pulled Gloria off of Daddy Pardon and led her beyond the clutter of trailers. They crossed the road into Acre Field where they turned and watched.

The preacher spilled his next shells around his feet and clawed in the mud for them. Six of Fen's winged neighbors rose into the air bearing their riders. Sterla was the last to leave the ground, her wings fighting the weight of her. Daddy Pardon staggered on his hands and knees, his wings torn and the final rider dead beside him.

Gloria wept and Fen hugged her to him. "I got us money," he told her, "we can go anyplace we want."

But she only sobbed in silence. Murray went on howling his mournful dissonance and the rain fell harder still. The preacher screamed his sermon until he went hoarse and was left to his own hell. The residents and their burdens circled the red spire beneath the opening in the clouds. They looked wondrous and somehow beautiful to Fen's eyes as he pressed Gloria beneath his chin. Her hair still smelled of dry old books even in the rain that darkened its orange.

"You want to go with them?" he said. Her face moved side to side against his chest. "What is it, then? Can you go north with me?" He felt her shoulders lift in a shrug. Even after the past ten minutes, he felt amazed that she had learned these gestures for him.

He stalled a moment before asking the next question. "Are you all angels who lost your wings?" She nodded her head this time and pulled away to gaze up at the others. "Are you supposed to go back?"

Yes, she nodded, and he thought of the vulgar ecstasies he'd heard in the darkness of the trailer park. He thought of what Hawk had said about sweetness and the taste of his woman. And he remembered the deep throbs of yearning for this girl, nestled beside her in his bed, the countless times he'd held back from touching the secret parts of her. Weeks of tamping down the roar of desire.

"You lost your wings and the only way to get home was from—from *being* with us all. In that way. You all *wanted* that?" Gloria turned to him at this and her nod was a ghost of a gesture. She tried to smile but it hardly touched her lips.

"Is there snow in heaven?" he asked her and she tilted her head in puzzlement. The others still flew in arcs around the spire as if waiting for Gloria and Fen to join them.

The world was a stranger to Fen but so was everything else. It could be that where Gloria came from held an allure of its own. He could finally see that from the first night she'd left the consummation to him. For when he was ready to love her. But now all droughts had ended.

He kissed her and the two of them were taken by greed. Their hands clutched and pulled. He unbuttoned his shirt but when he snatched at his belt she stopped him. *No*, she gestured and took his hands. Her head swept back and forth, *no* and *no*.

"But I want to go with you," he said.

Gloria smiled. She got it right this time and it awoke her entire face. She took his hand and tugged him toward the road, where she stood on the asphalt and pointed north. Murray barked once, a pronouncement. Fen smiled, kissed her again and they began to walk. An eagerness bloomed in him. Soon he was talking of buying an old car with their money, getting his license. He wondered about the many things they would see from its windows, his words running into one another in his excitement. He'd find a place for them where it got cold once in a while.

Above them the spire was now absent of orbiting angels. When it slipped from sight around a bend in the road, Fen did not notice the first cracks thread Gloria's face. They filled with blood that didn't quite wash away in the rain that still thrummed upon them there in the night. The whites of her eyes darkened as the road took them farther from her departed kin.

Before long the three travelers passed out of El Hueco. The boy grinned and walked with his hands in his pockets to protect the money they would need. The girl pushed herself on and tried to dredge strength from the song inside her. The hound shook his coat free of water only to soak again.

The Inconsolable

I didn't leave a note to say why but everybody knew. Early last month when I opened my eyes in the hospital there was a steady beeping over my head. My mother slapped me across the cheek. The hug she gave me after that hurt more. Pop sat in a chair against the wall and the lines in his face had been carved deeper. His hair had silvered a little brighter. A tube was rooted in my arm, a weightless moment when I felt it was feeding off me, but it was only the slow drip of living.

Em was in the room the next time I woke up. She'd been crying and mascara streaked under her eyes. She made me promise her it was a one-time thing and my tongue dried up in my mouth as I said it. I knew the small movements of her body. Every limb, her hips and the way she cupped an elbow in a palm said this didn't change anything. Her thighs never even touched the bed as she stood over me. She squeezed my fingers once, shook her head inside its sheaves of dark brown. Pressed her lips tight together and left all over again.

•

Each day as it comes, Pop says. The slow drip of living even with the tube gone. The nights black and the days flat and you can hardly care. A house was never so still and her smell lingers in everything. The TV snow sounds like rain. The sun at the window edges gets to be like fingers trying to pry in and you can't ever quite pull the curtain far enough over.

You just go on if God saw fit to spare you is how my mother puts it. He wouldn't like it if you clawed at Him until He dropped you. So you try and take some time to dump your life out on the coffee table and puzzle yourself back into one picture.

The morning crawls through to midday. Outside the start of October rusting the world, and sometimes of late black cutout birds gather strung on the power lines. Weeks now. Dozens and they don't move. I don't move. But a man's got to eat so I at last step down off the porch, tug the bill of my cap tight over my eyes and walk hunched to the van. The glare of the day makes the road a clean white sheet of paper. A new start, Mom would tell me. In town I buy the things my fingers touch, the things with fat and sugar. Em would have pitched a fit once.

I have tried to learn to think of her across a great distance. That space she stretched out between us. I do a bad job of it until it feels like I see her through a magnifying lens. A bearing rattles in a front wheel and I drive around a long time, making the rattle slowly worse, windows rolled down to the clean pine air, the inside of me like it's packed in mothballs.

Back home the sky's deepened to a blush, the sun lowered to a smudge of peach a thumb's width above the woods east of here. Far enough in those pines will take a man onto the toes of the Appalachians and on through the Carolinas to the ocean a dream away.

I pull in the driveway and get out of the van and the birds are still on the power lines. Both sides of the road now. I walk to the porch as more of them settle in a row along the roof peak. Little gaps and patterns between them like

Morse code.

Is this how it works, I almost ask them. Weighted down with portents as something draws close. Eyes black as their feathers, as holes. I stand on the porch. A gallon milk jug sweats against my hand. The crows or ravens are quiet and there are only the bugs dying out in the fall. My arm begins to ache and the night opens its jaws, slow and cool.

·

These days like sacks that need filling. Em was always my favorite pastime. I don't get paid vacations but I was asked to take a month and a half off starting with the day I swallowed the pills. In two Mondays I'll be back putting up aluminum siding in calm colors and keeping myself pieced together. I promised Em, wherever she is.

I get that thing about God my mother told me stuck in my head. I end up picking through the guest room closet for a picture she gave me one birthday. She can't seem to give up fighting Pop to give me religion. She swears I loved Jesus as a kid, so I had to have lost Him from my heart somewhere along the way.

I find the picture under some old towels. A postcard sun is setting over a postcard beach. The surf sprays the sand and across it all in shadowed letters is a poem called "Footprints in the Sand." There's a lonesome row of prints, still clear as though the feet that made them have just stepped out of the camera's eye. In the poem a man accuses Christ of abandoning him in the bleakest, blackest moments of his life, and Christ claims there is only the one set of footprints along the beach because it was He who carried the man through his sorrow.

Are You carrying me now, I ask, but not in words because I have never prayed since I was a small boy bowing his head and pretending. Am I slung across Your shoulders, and the only answer is the wash of the TV stuck between channels in the other room.

I watch the sifting screen and eat cereal so sugary my teeth are filmed by it after I drink the milk from the bowl. I step outside into a night with the streetlamps blotted, a dark that begins with me and blankets out to the edges of the earth. The moon is gone. There are no shadows but I see one anyway standing out by the mailbox watching me.

I go back in. Turn the deadbolt and start trying to sleep. I prop the poem on the night table and the red alarm clock light makes the ocean blood.

●

I keep thinking about the footprints. Sunday morning I dust off my black shoes in a box from the basement and find a Baptist church down the road. Just a one-room brick building far removed from the deep auditorium my family would worship in, almost too long ago to remember. It has a steeple tipped with a cross that seems bent except when I look right at it.

We sing low and drone hymns I don't know and somewhere one clear, sweet voice rings out through us like an angel trying to get home. I stare at Jesus and His downcast eyes follow me even though I don't move except to stand for the singing and sit for the preaching. He hangs defeated on the crucifix in the center of the wall above a faded piano. His body exhausted and at the very end of grievous suffering. His flesh wanting off His bones.

An old woman with hair that floats in a shimmery perm drops to the wine-colored carpet like a stone and amens ripple across the church. She lifts her arms and gazes at the blank ceiling. The preacher slides off his tie and opens his shirt two buttons and pounds a fist on the pulpit. He shouts damnation in a voice that bends the syllables, lifts the ends of sentences into half-questions. Slick with sweat he pauses for long slugs of water from a crystal pitcher and thick foam begins to gather at the corners of his mouth.

The light in the church seems to pale and brighten and become separated into nimbuses around certain heads of the people lined up in the pews. The true believers or maybe just the lucky.

I wait for warmth around my own face. I want to feel that light against my hair. A man with jowls and beautiful green eyes comes to me and asks if I am saved. He places a hand on my shoulder and puts his weight into it. I don't know, I tell him, and he leads me to an altar below the pulpit and I kneel leaned over with my fingers splayed on its worn cushion. The man gets on his knees beside me, a soft thud in the floor beneath him. And I bow my head and try to pray. I picture the birds on the roof and if Christ cannot carry me, could they?

*

My parents bookend me on the couch and Mom says that getting back to work will be good for me. I tell her I went to church to try and be saved and her eyes fill with tears. Her face collapses with joy and I watch her worries flake away. She looks almost young underneath. Pop grunts and looks down at his fists.

She wants to know if Jesus touched my heart. The bones in her hand wrap around my knee. Maybe He did, I answer, but I'm not sure yet.

Pop says I should come over soon for beers and baseball playoffs and they leave lighter than when they came in. Their car slides past the line of trees and around a curve and the birds fill up the sky as if they have been waiting. They grasp the power lines and the roof and the luggage rack of my van with their perfect little centers of gravity.

I peer across the road and the wide shallow field. Someone is walking behind the pines out there. A figure in a white dress moving slowly to the right, the rough trunks cutting its passage into a rhythm. Their straw-bunched limbs rustle far above. My heart beats to catch up.

I feel a bird land on my shoulder and I turn my head into its depthless eyes. A crow, I think, not a raven. Needles prick my skin through my shirt and I wonder if it will try to lift me. Its beak flashes out and there's a sting at my temple and blood running down my cheek. I try to knock the crow away. It shakes its wings and takes flight toward the white walker. They both vanish into the trees.

A heat blooms around my head and the sky pulses. I blink many times until I'm sure the woods are empty.

•

Em drifted away from me slow as a continent. So slow she still felt close until the night she sat me down two months ago and said she loved me just as much but not in the way she had. It was a long time coming, she told me, since before she decided against our baby growing inside of her. It was natural and it would nurture our lives if we were apart. Across the room her ring caught the light from the kitchen counter and a tan line had taken its place on her finger. It didn't matter what I said back.

I came home the next day and her part of us was all in boxes slashed with black marker strokes. We only saw each other once more before the hospital. I don't remember what I said to her then either. She had the end of her things in her car and the walls were full of vacant nails. It was one of the last hot days with sweat all over me just from the helplessness of my words I now forget.

•

My eyes open into the blue black of the bedroom. The windows would welcome the soft fall another night but now they're shut against a rain that still washes the house. I know something has woken me up. There's no pain in my bladder and the clock says thirty-three past two.

A tap comes at the window that looks out over the front yard and the road. I roll my head on the pillow and a face is staring in through the rivers that run down the glass and join together into sheets of water. A long pale face with hanging ropes of hair behind the rain, eyes wide and mouth opened up and pressed against the window. The water makes it like seeing through a lens, the way I see Em sometimes, but it looks like a man. I think the teeth are what rapped against the glass until the tongue darts out. It strikes once then again and the window cracks into a small web. The face draws back and is gone and only the steady whisper of rain is left.

I sleep on the couch with the snow on the TV mixing together with the rain into a quiet roar.

In the morning the windowpane is broken out, the wet curtain breathing in the wind. I look for footprints along the floor but there is only a puddle. Before breakfast I dial Em's number by heart but like every day it is still disconnected.

•

At church again the sermon is about someone named Lot who sounds familiar and I raise my hand and ask if we can hear about the footprints in the sand. Heads all turn to stare at me and from their looks I know I'm not supposed to interrupt.

The preacher clears his throat, sips water poured from the crystal pitcher and remembers me from the past week when I was saved. I tell him and the staring crowd with its lowered eyebrows I don't know if I was saved but I'm interested in finding out. And I say that my fiancée doesn't love me anymore and maybe it would be helpful to be carried by Jesus a while.

The preacher asks what was my name again and I tell him Alden and after a moment he says that just for me next week we'll talk about the footprints.

I pray at the altar some more and ask for help keeping my promise to Em. For a second I feel something inside. Then it's just the same hollow space but I think that I am close to being saved.

The preacher finishes about Lot and a pillar of salt and God raining destruction upon the wicked and the lost. Jesus stares at the carpet from His cross so that we don't have to. We sing hymns and that clear, honeyed voice in the congregation is missing today.

*

On the way to visit my folks I stop for gas and see Em standing at a pump holding a little boy's hand. She bends down and the boy laughs into her face. I put the van in park along the curb in front of a payphone that has just an empty cord hanging down the front of it. I slide low in the seat and stare over the door. A strange moment pulls itself out and I wonder if maybe she lied to me and didn't go to that clinic one morning and come back blank and faraway. I wonder if years have somehow passed. But then a man steps into view and kisses the side of Em's head. He's taller than I am next to her and his hair is graying. A tightness draws in my chest and I can't breathe. I can almost feel the tube back in my arm.

The boy climbs up into the car and Em shuts the door. The man holds her hips and her arms slip around his neck and they kiss. I know the small movements of her body. I watch them until they leave.

The van could run out of gas but I pull back out onto

the road and drive away toward my parents in the opposite direction. I rock back and forth and calm myself by picturing one line of footprints on a beach filling up with foamy water. I drive slow and mumble what snatches of hymns I've learned.

*

Mom says I will know when I am saved and to not worry until then. Jesus finds the sorrowful. I walk through their house and look at all the pictures of Him in the rooms Pop doesn't care about. Over my old bed He sits atop a large rock holding a lamb and surrounded by children. His hair curls down onto His shoulders and the robe He wears is a clean white that almost glows. I stand a long time looking at it and think about what He might be saying to the children.

We eat a casserole and I don't remember who won the baseball game as soon as it is over. I drink two beers but they only make me tired and soon I am driving back under a sky that has too many stars in it.

The birds are waiting. They have spread to the grass and the porch railing and click against the gutters above. They regard me as I unlock the door and look around but there's no one in the house. The weight of that drags me down onto the couch. I say out loud that I am just too weary for it all. I pray and the words go deeper than they did in church. On top of the beers I fall asleep more quickly than I have in weeks.

*

Sometime in the night breath puffs on my skin and I look up. Jesus is leaning over me close enough to feel the cold off Him. His eyes wet with oil are set deep in the chalk white face. They open up into holes black as the birds. The mouth

I saw through the window unhinges wide and inside at the back of it the tongue twitches between thin crowded teeth.

I look at Him. I swear my heart is frozen shut as His long fingers of sharpened bone press to my chest and squeeze. I must open my heart to Him. He doesn't speak but His voice is a sweet murmur somewhere between the sound of rain in the TV and the church angel singing. His hair hangs down full of leaves and pine needles. The white robe stained brown and gray flows to His ankles. He smells of deep rich dirt.

His eyes weep onto me and the tears run to my lips. I lick with my tongue and there is no salt in them. The voice says nothing but in it I am told of mercy. A finger traces along my jaw and down my neck, over each button of my shirt and back to my heart.

I am the inconsolable. Come, His yoke is easy, and His burden light. He kneels before the coffee table. He has turned His back on me. I let out a small wounded moan and I hear His fingernails scrape the glass top of the table. But then I understand. I climb up onto my knees and circle my arms around His neck. He stands and He is so tall. I push off the couch and swing my legs out to hook around His waist and feel His backbone press into me like hard river stones.

And Jesus carries me through the dark room and opens the door to the sound of a thousand wings ruffling. He steps off the porch into a beating cloud of black that coats the air and covers the sky.

His feet cross the lawn, leaving one set of prints sunk into the earth. There is no light, not a drop of it around His head, as the road is behind us and the high grass parts through the field and the woods full of pines swallow us up.

Dancers

Since the exorcism it's been Mae who can't sleep. The lights, which no longer flicker and buzz in the night, have been clicked off. Her husband stretches himself out near the middle of the bed, clean-souled and unmindful of her space. Ellis snored every night of their twenty-eight years, until Father Darcy cast the devil out of his mouth. Now there is quiet, and the question of what to do with it.

She spends so much of her time in this bed now, light crawling down walls into dark and a faint sourness rising from the unwashed sheets. Her bones have been heavy with a—not a sickness, it is more like a blight that slowly expands. Her bones have been heavy with the weight of her marriage, too: how they got here, where here is. It rained earlier and she caught herself reveling in the variance of it.

Those showers tapered an hour ago, and perhaps the moon is full and blurred with humidity above the house. Mae has lost track of its phases and can't bring herself to look, fearful she might do other things if she gets out of bed, starting with the jar on the high shelf in the pantry. She fixes her eyes on the ceiling instead, toward the moon, until Ellis falls into his depthless sleep, then turns onto her side to watch the two oaks entwine in the side yard. She feels herself

131

come to the very edge of crying.

Four weeks gone and still she can't stop picturing the black tangle of worms Ellis coughed onto his chest that cloudless, sun-choked afternoon in July. It seems to call to her from the kitchen, down the hall. Colored whispers. She hears them even as she stares out the window, at the dancers.

These two Japanese live oaks ended up being their only children. It's a strange thought to keep coming back to at her age—that they never got around to adopting. Never got around, like it was a chore, an attic that needed insulating. Looking back, it feels like a version of herself that rose once with a shout, then calmly passed on. Where did that Mae go? But after they gave up and stopped trying to conceive, somewhere around their tenth anniversary (Ellis gave her the loveliest filigreed box handmade from tin), she still had her hopes: in the gesture of adoption, in the handful of brochures. But not where it counted. Her heart took its time healing. She thinks of how children are a way of marking your life, cultivating their growth while keeping your attention away from what your own body is doing to you, busy winding down into itself. A selfish act, having children, she's always told herself this. Without them she has been her own vessel.

She doesn't understand this resurgent ache. It's an empty, clenching hurt that would have faded a decade ago even for a woman with a virile husband. Life has no choice but to go on, she has found. As everyone finds. But this feels sharper even than it did in her forties. The last time she went to the market, a few days after the exorcism, Mae was caught following a woman through the produce section, weaving with her around the long troughs of plump vegetables, pausing with her to squeeze the avocados. The woman asked Mae to stop staring at her belly, but Mae couldn't. It hung there, swollen with child. Mae's hand reached out to cup that great curve, then a manager was summoned and Mae

high stones near the tree line. If the world is hushed you can hear Vintner Creek whispering in the distance back in the woods, near the Stillwell property. She didn't know where he got the stones, uniformly shaped things, like worn teeth. Ellis would stand in the circle in the evening and stare into the trees, and Mae asked him more than once, with a shaky laugh, wasn't this fire pit he was building a little big?

The smell of him turned to spoiled meat, turned to something darker and deeper. But she enjoyed taking care of him, and she kept letting herself not call a doctor. The hot days of strange, lush moaning, the foul language in overlaid voices, the gouged skin, bleeding orifices—these are things that have dispersed into unpleasant memories. He was fine, after. The trouble is that Mae feels caught in their wake. The whispers from the kitchen find the gap under the bedroom door. She can have children. It's not too late for them. Maybe a family would even fix everything that's gone. She looks out the window with her eyes closed.

Ellis is awake, it seems. He rolls toward her and the warmth of him pushes against her. And she feels sure that his eyes are open, staring at her, maybe watching the scant angle of moonlight catch the gray hairs she stopped counting a long time ago. She knows his eyes are still and wide, the small muscles around them taut with awareness. In a displacement of air she senses his hand lift out of the covers and hang above her shoulder. Her own muscles, the ones in her back, twitch in a horrible anticipation of his touch.

Her thoughts drag across the span of their marriage. They shift in time and these regrets and strange shapes emerge from the cracks, like things glimpsed between sliding plates in the earth.

He knew how to wait. It took patience to shape the trees. Mae remembers the day he came home with a box of small glass ornaments, each the size of a tennis ball. Thin eggshells filled with a secret air. The oaks only reached a child's height then, a child that might have been used to waiting for the bus on her own but still would need some source of light to sleep. The trunks narrow as collapsed umbrellas, still not the young trees that would find their quiet majesty.

From the corner of the house, near the Adirondack chairs, she watched him hang the ornaments from the limbs, arranging them as an artist might, moving the red and green balls an inch here, imperceptibly there. He nestled them next to the anchors of the sparse leaves. When he was finished, the two saplings looked like postmodern Christmas trees, each laden with five ornaments, positioned so that they bowed toward each other. Ellis wrapped electrical tape across the hooks to add the right weight and hold them in place, and he waited.

"What are you doing?" she asked.

"Teaching them," he said.

The priest was forced upon their home. Their neighbor, Mr. Parker, elderly and nosy as his namesake, called his church after Ellis spent ten minutes half-howling, half-chanting at the sunrise one morning. The old man claimed he'd found the heads of his two cats wedged into the chain-link fence that ran across the bottom of his property line. Mr. Parker had never struck Mae as the type to bypass the police in favor of spiritual guidance, but Father Darcy came the next evening, clutching his Bible and drenched with sweat the moment he saw the tendrils of smoke rising from Ellis's skin as he sat on the couch. "This man is in trouble," he told Mae. And now she can't remember what she said to that. But she let him stay, and she led Ellis down the hall and helped Father Darcy tie her husband to the bed.

Mae still feels Ellis's eyes behind her. On her. It would be good to think he, too, is looking out at the oaks. She remembers the priest's Bible shaking in his hand when it was done, and all the blood fled from his face as he watched the squirming mass in the V of Ellis's t-shirt. The devil looked something like a smoker's lung unraveled into strips of thriving tissue. Two white eyes opened in its center, widened at her, then several of its many wet protuberances lifted up the cotton to crawl inside the shirt. Mae knocked it to the floor, and not until she threw the bed sheet over it did she realize she was screaming. When she silenced herself, the devil spoke to her. Those bright whispers. Ellis, his face coated with a viscous, sooty saliva, had already drifted into unconsciousness when she turned and went to him.

And she remembers—she makes herself remember how she stood over him with a washcloth, feeling the summer air through the open windows of the bedroom, the wet weight of tears rimming her eyelashes, relieved, shaking with relief, and feeling—? What was it she felt? A letting go. A small bereavement at odds with his survival. She cleaned his face, gently as he slept, and mourned something. When she was finished, she threw the washcloth in the trash and came back with an old Mason jar. She told Father Darcy she was going to burn the thing, then looked out at the dancers until the priest's old boat of a car passed beyond them and down the street.

Over the years Ellis narrowed his focus to the trunks and two limbs of each tree. He began tying clothesline to them and pinning the lines in the earth, a gradual web of precise angles. She admired the way he stepped back each time and took in the geometry, moved forward to adjust the tow of a limb, the bow of a trunk. The oaks grew stout and what had once supported dozens of fragile ornaments, multiplying like fruit, now boasted a set of small iron balls hung in cloth slings. And when he began trimming, with office scissors, not shears, Mae began to see what he had been doing all along. She wept not with the beauty of it but with the few minutes a day he had pooled into such a great lake of sentiment for her.

She visits the oaks, touches their bark most days, in tribute to his effort. But it's difficult, losing herself in a tableau that's always there. The trees have become furniture, like the comforts of her marriage. Their curves seem to hold the exact shape of her sight. She's watched them on nights that were sleepless for many other reasons. Solicitude, distance, a waning of momentum that often felt like a shadow yawning toward her. She watched these oaks as Father Darcy spent two hours chanting himself hoarse at the thing that had nested in her husband. She went outside and sat beneath them as the priest dribbled holy water in lines across Ellis, drawing the devil out like wasp venom. It seems she is always watching them. Still looking out.

What Ellis did, across those years, was fashion the oaks into two ballroom dancers. He never coaxed them into looking like humans. There was simply the suggestion that let the eyes fill in the details, and for that she always loved him, or tried to keep loving him when the tenor of her heart changed. They are still trees, trees that have only, always, just realized themselves and are on the cusp of reveling in it. The man (so called by Mae, as he features a small knob in his trunk near chest height) grasps the woman's outstretched right limb with his left, and his right loosely circles her trunk. The female has a hollow at ground level, shallow, more like a pocket, but it's far too low to facilitate the sexual imagery. Each regards its partner with a stately aloofness, green crowns tipped back at a slight angle. On the grand verge of beginning, and again Mae fits her whole adult life into the mold of this observation.

Ellis as a young man: earnest, blond and feather-haired, nearly hairless swimmer's body. She misses gliding her palms down his chest, feeling them dip down in a quick dive into the taut curls of pubic hair. She misses dumb laughter and pots of tea and shower sex, her face pressed against tile grout as he rocked behind her. She misses the unexciting road trips, the desktop globe he dotted with thumbtacks they would visit one day, some day that kept drifting around the curve of the earth ahead of them.

Ellis as a middle-aged man: diligent, balding, new moles breeding like lint across a doughy paunch. A spirit of adventure that reaches no farther than the link of a clothesline tied to an oak's limb. It's not that she doesn't have her own stubborn pockets of fat, or that her breasts haven't felt the pull of age and its gravity. But she's lost the Mae who wasn't supposed to worry about things sagging. The Mae who wanted her lover, who didn't have to think about that wanting. The one who wanted the things she was able to have.

For a moment, a glimmer of a moment, she hoped the devil would take certain things of Ellis with it, trailing them like viscera. Hollow him out, leave a cavity of hope behind. But since the exorcism it's been Mae who's not herself.

The bed shifts with a creak deep in its coils, and his breath spreads on the back of her neck. She goes rigid, curls the sheet in a fist. If she gets out of the bed, it could cleave the dynamic that's left to them here. Mae asks herself again why they never adopted a child. Two children. Like everyone else, she wanted a boy and a girl. This question seems to be where all the weight has gone.

She feels his stomach push against her before his hand grasps her hipbone. "Mae," he says, just Ellis and his one flat Kansas voice. He tugs on her and his lips touch her neck. Some wicked part of her wishes for his tongue to swipe across her skin. "You have to get past this. You have to go back to work." The words are cold there against the imprint his mouth left. "Please talk to me, honey."

She surprises herself by sliding away and finding her feet. It's been days or even weeks since she thought about work. How is that possible? Janice won't let her come back after nearly a month of silence. Mae's restaurant clients have surely found other consultants. But it passes out of her mind again, as her eyes find the trees again. May I have this dance, the oak closest to the fence and Fremont Street has asked. You may, the other has said, always a moment ago, never quite in the past. Mae stands at the window. Everything is stilled in time.

"Our life never moved," she says. Her breath gives her a small field of fog on the windowpane in which to write a solution, if she had one. Slowly she wonders if, maybe, she might. "I'm fifty-two years old and you rooted me in the same dirt as your trees. Such an obvious metaphor. I don't know why I thought your...spiritual cleansing would change that."

"Mae, I—"

"No, you may not," she says, and turns around to smile at him, to show him the old rueful pun. "I loved us so much, Ellis. I used to love the way you made us."

And with his false starts at the right words fading after her, Mae leaves the room and nearly floats down the hallway lined with framed photographs that don't have people in them. A shuttered gas station outside of Omaha, power lines heavy with crows; an abandoned trailer park; the Grand Canyon; things that are empty, pictures she doesn't know if she or Ellis took. Each must have felt like a moment at the time.

She passes into the kitchen, where she opens the pantry and steps up onto the folding stool. On tiptoes, from behind boxes of dry goods, she lifts out the Mason jar. Ellis calls her name from the bedroom as she lowers herself to the floor.

Stop all this endless thinking and turning over of old things. The devil stares through the glass at Mae, its eyes— black irises swimming in white sclera—full of words she shouldn't ever want to hear. The eyes blink to show her they might be something like human. A door or a veil opens in her mind and through it she sees two children crouching in the mud. The stones that ring them have grown taller, into monoliths, since Ellis planted them there behind the house in June. The girl and boy raise their trembling arms in some kind of rapture. They press their wrists against their temples, fingers splayed, then turn as one and stare back between the stones and through the door at Mae. They're both such seamless blends of her and Ellis that her heart aches.

She is pushing the back door open before she realizes she has moved at all. Ellis is still repeating her name somewhere behind her, and the night is ripe with stars. She finds the moon, which isn't full, unless half of it is tucked into a slot in the sky, like a worn coin in an album. The jar hums in her hands for the first time since she scooped the devil inside it after the exorcism, and her voice wants to boil out of her. Some lizard in her wants to scream at the night.

The priest asked them to read the Bible during their nightly affirmations, and they nodded at him. They don't own a Bible. Ellis grew up thumping one, he's told her a thousand times, and Mae's parents lapsed long before she was born. She wonders now if there are words on those onionskin pages that would have guided her someplace else. Or if she would still be here, holding this jar. The ring of standing stones is now a huddled, pocket Stonehenge, and Mae has to close her eyes and open them again to bring the two children back. They're watching her but pretending not to, smiling down at the wet earth. Are they wearing antlers? She can't tell. She can't say anything. The air is thick and hot and wavering, a sort of passion welling in it.

She can see the dancers, off to the right beside the house. The bending rim of the sky seems to drop stars into their crowns. She remembers the day Ellis presented them to her, as though she hadn't witnessed their slow metamorphosis alongside him. They'd stood beside the trees that day and held their opening pose, mirroring them, laughing. And there were evenings, the sun draining into the woods behind them, that they did dance, and she's sure they smiled and pressed their warm skins together.

Mae turns back to watch the boy and girl gently spasm in the mud. She realizes she's close to naked, though the night is cool and she remembers wearing her pajamas to bed. *Let me out,* the devil says, and she does. The lid unscrews as if greased and disappears into grass that hasn't been cut since midsummer.

The children wink out in a sigh and Mae staggers after them into the circle of stones, which seem taller than she is now. She pulls the devil out of the jar, feeling its spongy flesh swell and pulse in her hand, its worms twining around her wrist. It tells her where her children are and how to find them. Mae is nodding as Ellis bangs out of the house toward her, in only his underwear, and there's a moment where she sees the wonderful, gorgeous man he was, hidden in the pasty bulk. Then she simply wishes he had a shirt on so she wouldn't have to see the meat of him bounce as he runs across the yard.

She drops the jar to where her feet have sunk into the mud. She strips her panties off and a deeper chill clasps her skin. *Let me in*, the devil says, and Mae spreads her legs. The fingers of her left hand pull her cleft open. The fingers of her right hand lower the devil to her secret heat.

"God, Mae! Stop that!" Ellis says from miles away. Behind that veil she hears the truth whispered as the thing's appendages trace the insides of her thighs. This is no devil writhing in her hand, wanting her. It reveals to her that it is a visitor. The seed of something much older. Its age and the distance it has traveled send a throb through her sex. She places it against the opening and slips it in, just as Ellis's hand comes down on her wrist, knocking the thing back out, and they both fall into the mud inside the stones.

"Stop it!" Mae doesn't know who's screaming these two words over and over. She's fighting him, she grasps his cock and twists in anger. Ellis screams into the mud. The thing from the jar is squirming near his head.

"I'll put it back in me!" Ellis says, rising and struggling to pin her arms to the ground. "I'll kill it. I'll find a way to be rid of it. Please, honey. You have to quit this." He's panting, holding her down. And the door shuts in Mae's head. The veil tumbles back. She calms, goes limp, and she doesn't know why.

"Ellis," she says, and grabs the sides of his face. "Ellis." She kisses him and he tries to turn away from her. "Ellis."

"You don't know what it was, having that inside me," he says. They sit up, stare back toward the house. "Why on earth did you keep it?"

"So I could keep the earth, is why." And she laughs at the thought of the little girl in *The Exorcist* speaking backward.

"What do you mean?"

"You mean the world to me." The reason she's calm now——Mae watches the seed, spent from some faraway god, burying itself in the mud, but now she feels the age of her body. By her own standards, she is as ancient. She leans forward and digs it out, then gets to her feet. The thing has stilled in her fingers, as though dreaming. Somewhere in her mind she thinks of the pregnant woman at the market, the overripe avocado Mae burst between her fingers, unknowing, as she stared at the distended belly. She lets go of something she supposes she never did before. But it doesn't explain why they never adopted.

She turns to ask Ellis, but she knows what he would say if he was aware of his answer. It comes down to seeds. Instead she walks out of the ring of stones, back toward the house. Their two tall children stand guard, and she goes to them and traces a finger around the knob of the male's trunk. She thinks of all Ellis's work, his slow guidance. She thinks of how they still don't know how he got the devil inside him. And she remembers the tight cords that were once tied to the trees' arms and necks, pulling them into place. What if those cords had drifted into the sky instead of being pinned to the earth? She's never thought of the oaks as marionettes before, but the image blooms in her—up there, hands she can't fathom twitching at strings, like plucking instruments.

Ellis might have gone back inside the house, or collapsed in the mud. She doesn't see him or the children inside the stones. The sky grows darker, the stars pulling back from her into a deep black. The seed wants her. She feels it even as it dreams. But it's been left up to her.

Up to her—she digs at the hollow space in the female tree's trunk, just above where the roots spread like legs. And she realizes the tree's womb has always been in the perfect place. It's the male's knob that is out of true.

One last time she gazes at the seed. "How many of you are here among us?" she asks it. In response she feels images coalesce into an alien language in the center of her brain, painful, unfolding kernels that almost speak, *More. Many.* Yellow holes in a low sky, drooling rain. Vast eyes peering through them. The hinted gleam of metal or scaled hulls. She can't pretend to know what she's seeing or the words inside it. Her tongue and her eyes are crossed wires, but there comes the sense of—

—Mae is choosing to give to another, more receptive vessel this immense knowledge, this rethreading of synapses. The sperm comes awake, the worms of it exploring the loose soil. Its eyes watch her, calm and trusting. Mae slips it inside the oak's hollow and pushes a mound of dirt in after it.

Now she wants to sleep. But first she finds Ellis, sitting in an Adirondack chair by the back door, his head in his hands. "What are you doing to the trees?" he asks her.

"Teaching them," she says.

She takes him into the shower and lets him clean her. He grows hard and fumbles behind her as she braces herself against the tiled wall, the water passing from clotted brown to clear into the drain. She doesn't come, but she hasn't in ages and the lack of it has no teeth tonight. She finds herself wondering if fifty-two is too late to visit an adoption agency. After, they put their pajamas back on, demure and buttoned all the way, and Mae tells him the ring of stones will stand through the night. She tells herself the boy and girl she saw inside the stones will not.

The bed is warm. They might have never left it. She looks through the window at the only children they managed to have, and some time later one of them moves, finally into the first step of the dance. The oak shakes her sculpted crown and straightens her spine. Mae waits to see what the dance will be. It could be a waltz. It could be a violent breaking of her mate's limbs, a long straining of her fibrous tendons, knees bending, as her roots extract from the pulp of the ground, as she sets off on her agenda, the harbinger with green grace, of yellow mouths opening somewhere now closer above them.

A Thousand Hundred Years

"Tu hija te espera."

Ms. Onwe's words echoed his dream, for a moment drew it into the dim hallway with him. Jandro hadn't noticed the tiny old woman just behind her door, cataracts holding the hall light like wet pearls. He must have misheard her. She would have told him in the past year if she knew any Spanish. Even her half-broken English lapsed at times into Mandarin, where her voice stretched out to poetry.

"What do you mean, my daughter is waiting for me?" he said, hearing the angry waver in his voice. She was going soft, but she wouldn't say something so cruel to a man whose four-year-old child was missing. He'd lived next door to Ms. Onwe since he and Krista fell apart and he became a weekend dad. They always chatted when he passed her open door, and Virginia had loved her. He had far less to say these days, but she liked to fill the new silences with tokens of sympathy—musty Taiwanese books, chipped tea mugs. Jandro was touched that a hoarder would surrender anything to him.

"They are no dreams you have, Mr. Jandro," the old woman said, her withered face peering up toward his shoulder. "You need my projector. I hear the movies of your daughter through your wall at night. I hear you cry."

"Movies?" he said. "Your projector?"

She smiled and her white eyes came closer into the light. "No need to see Chun-chieh and Chih-ming travel on my wall any longer."

Her dead sons, she meant. Presumed dead, anyway. They had been flying home to Taiwan three years ago. The plane had disappeared halfway across the Pacific, but it had never been found, she'd told him many times. Jandro had learned enough for a good rough sketch of her, listening through the chores he helped with. She'd come to the States in the nineties, her husband had been gone almost as long, and her apartment stank of those two packrat decades.

He found himself almost grateful to put Virginia out of his mind for a moment. Almost. His throat clenched for the handle of rye in his coat, the oblivion and the recurring dream of her that followed each day of aimless searching, peering into the corners of Delmar, turning over the same rocks. After the liquor store he'd spent longer than usual at the playground, his sobbing vigil in the clown's head, pretending two little hands were on the verge of pushing him down the slide. Krista had refused to update him on the police investigation for more than a week now. Her threats of reporting him to Immigration had gained weight. And while Detective Swinson had yet to say the word *suspect* to Jandro, the implication still hung over his questions, not quite dissipating.

He followed the old woman inside. "I can take it to a pawn shop, if it's worth something." She slipped into the deeper shadows, so he waited at the opening to her living room, the silhouettes of her hoard crowding the small space like a cave of strange teeth. "Or give it to Goodwill."

Preferably the dump, he thought, along with all these sagging things. The place violated every fire code in the book.

"I want you to see it, not store." Her voice came from somewhere to the right, followed by a sharp click. An orange-brown light fell from a shaded lamp, landing in a smear that hardly cut into the labyrinth of junk.

"Well, we never really had a camera, and Virginia—" He stopped. Because he couldn't get the rest out, and because Ms. Onwe was crouched down behind the lamp. Watching him, one milky eye peering around a square bulk that sat on an end table.

Jandro used his feet as antennae, boot toes brushing cardboard boxes and newspapers and humps concealed in garbage bags. She was no longer behind the projector when he reached her. She stood straight as a rail now, closer than he'd thought, her silver-threaded hair turned brass in the lamplight. Her sons smiled out of the shadows from a large photograph on the wall.

"You take," she whispered, and laid a pruned finger on his hand. He felt the finger bone roll inside the sleeve of loose skin. Her mouth seemed about to spread into an inexplicable grin. He looked away.

The projector was brushed steel, shaped a bit like a trumpeting elephant with reels attached to the trunk and rear. Jandro touched the cool metal, finding the open design beautiful and too honest.

He lifted it. There was a bad moment when it nearly slipped from his arms, because its size and weight reminded him of Virginia when she was a baby. *You're getting heavy, En*, he heard himself say just seven weeks ago, and his little girl hugged his windpipe shut before squirming to be let down, her Spanish lessons trailing back from her in sharp puffs of vapor. He blinked the thought away, leaned the projector back into the seam of his arm and chest.

"Do you know where Virginia is?" he asked Ms. Onwe.

She was so short it felt almost like giving En his stern daddy stare. She looked up at the picture of her sons. Jandro waited but that hot needle of alarm wasn't in his heart. She often made little sense—today was one more example—but he was sure she would have already shared anything close to helpful.

"No, Mr. Jandro," she said, still looking at the photograph. Watching it, somehow. "I should not say like that. I know what it is to lose children. And to wait." She touched his hand again. "Please, take." That rolling finger bone, its gentle insistence.

*

He enjoyed the same haze of whiskey, but the dream changed. Redrew its lines. Jandro came out of the woods a few seconds earlier than before, almost soon enough to reach his daughter. His life was full of almost. He watched En float away into the long pale sky, a bright smudge from which her yellow coat tumbled back to the earth like a shed skin. But now, all around him, a dozen or more Virginias lifted off the ground, the sleeves of those fallen coats reaching up for the arms that had filled them.

He thought he could hear their voices, but the cellophane static of radios drowned the words. Behind him, vaguely, was the sense of pursuit. The crackling of transmissions and dead pine needles. The cops were rounding up Mexicans all across this dream Delmar.

A shadow, pooling on the grass beside him. A looming hand. The INS badge gleamed as he was jerked around and a voice growled, "Alejandro de Garza, you are under arrest. *Tu mamá te espera.*"

His shoulder ached under that hand. But he could only crane his neck, watch his daughter—more than a dozen daughters, now—borne away into the sky. He could only wake. The waking was the awful thing.

*

Eight times on the slide. Eight or nine. The real question was how many seconds he'd spent checking his phone that morning. He had no memory of what the email or Facebook post had been. All it took were those few moments with his eyes somewhere else. But he kept trying to count her loops anyway, like picking a lock, eight or nine times on the slide.

They'd had the playground to themselves so early and cold on a Saturday morning. En had insisted. She ran for the swings first, the stubborn dark tangles of her hair bouncing, and Jandro sent her just high enough for a four-year-old to pretend the sky was too close as it fell toward her. "*Cielo, tierra, cielo, tierra*," she chanted. She wasn't learning Spanish anymore at home, so he tried to coax it into her the two days a week he had her.

She always saved the slide for last but could never wait long. The play structure was a giant clown's head, red hat and faded white face, and she loved it as much as it creeped Jandro out. There was a rhythm to her then that he'd memorized across a long string of weekends. The thuds of her sneakers up the ladder, her fisherman-yellow coat crinkling as she shifted into just the right spot, the lift of her voice into a half-squeal down the other side, and the slow whisk of plastic against the butt of her favorite pink corduroys. Repeat. Repeat. Watch me, Papá. Watch me, Daddy. And he had, most times he'd been happy to.

Eight slides. Or nine. She'd taken countless trips down it in the year after she and Krista had left him, it was their Daddy-En Saturday morning ritual along with their secret doughnut breakfast, but you couldn't always hold them in your eyes. There were cracks in time when you saw a pretty young mom with a stroller. When you looked up at a gliding

151

hawk, distant as a mote in a cloud's eye, or rooted for a wet wipe thinking her runny nose might need it. All those times you sat there on a bench thumbing your phone screen. Because you always knew the sound of your little girl's voice and the loop she made, up, settle, down, run back around.

And when the rhythm of her had cut off that morning, suddenly not there, Jandro looked up and saw right away that the playhouse was empty. The purple slide that came out of it like a bruised tongue, the ladder up into the clown's head, empty.

Behind him had been the drowsy street. Ahead, the wide, short field beyond the playground with only faded grass waiting for spring. The brief postscript of woods lay beyond it, but her little legs could never have reached them in the moment he'd looked at his phone. En loved those trees, liked to make Daddy hold his breath when they walked through them from the apartment building, because the air was poison and would make him fall asleep for a thousand hundred years.

He'd stood up into that breathless quiet and called her name, Virginia, Virginia. Her second word as a baby had been to pluck En out of the center of that mouthful, and Jandro only called her Virginia in scolds, or in the cold moment every daddy hoped would never, ever come.

She was gone. An image, cobbled together from all the fears that live in the backs of parents' minds—his daughter with a greasy hand clamped over her mouth, dragged into the trees, into the alley across Milton Ave., into dark places full of implacable horrors. He played his mental En-tape back. The last thing had been the sound of her shoes climbing back up the ladder. All the looks he got later, all the detectives' questions, the ringing in his eardrums after Krista's screams, wouldn't change that. There had been no child predator, no dirty fingers groping her, stealing her away. She hadn't gone down the slide that last time. Up the ladder, and there the loop of her hung broken in his mind, calling out its echo.

.

He opened his eyes, still drunk, and saw something in the room with him, a low black lump in the center of the studio apartment near the kitchen island. He and the shape waited in the dark together, Jandro swallowing his daughter's name, swallowing it again, finally whispering, "Ms. Onwe?"

It did not answer. Jandro thought he saw other shapes, sliding out of the bathroom doorway, crawling into the far corner of the ceiling above the refrigerator. There came a dry snapping sound, a metallic click, repeated several times. Like a light switch, a blown bulb. Quiet spread. He drifted off until it was morning, flat winter white and bruising cold.

He woke and scanned the apartment for detritus from his visitor. For a long moment he stood in the middle of the single room, shivering, trying to decide if it had been a new dream.

The door was locked, but the window was open several inches. Outside it was wet enough for the snow to clump together before it landed twenty feet below. He checked today's fresh line of footprints leading away from the apartment building to the trees, the park beyond them. He'd learned not to trust those prints, though they were small and shallow enough. They could belong to anyone's kid—the building had three or four around toddler age that he knew of. And the tracks filled so fast in all the snow. His heart ached to think of spring, when this strange trail would be gone, too.

He closed the window and leaned his forehead against the pane, relishing the cold, willing it to tighten the blood vessels in his brain. A quick breakfast shot of whiskey handled most of the headache, but he could never shake it all off.

He had to find work. Mr. Callum at Daye Construction had hated to let him go. He'd had five good years with Daye, solid work and respectable pay, and as an illegal you didn't just let something like that slip away. But he'd been a drunken wreck after that morning at the playground. A month later he'd been even worse, without even the pretense of showing up at the job sites.

Of course En was probably—he came closer to thinking the word than usual, but still couldn't allow it. But he understood the near inevitability. And his mother's lymphoma wasn't going to cure itself, her slow death back in Puebla. He hadn't had the heart to call her once since Virginia had gone missing. She had never even met her granddaughter, and he couldn't bear to tell her she never would. So here he was, losing his mamá, too, in all of this. He was missing the end of her life, two and a half thousand miles away in Delaware.

But she needed an influx of cash that he was running out of. He had to work. This crusade was grinding to a bitter end.

The projector stood on the granite island that, flanked by two barstools, served as his counter space and dining table. It was a simple model: a few knobs and toggle switches, a lens with a focus dial around it. An odd nub protruded from the back of the machine, covered with foil mesh. MICR had been written below it with a felt pen. He stretched the cord over to the counter and plugged it in beside the toaster.

A powerful urge to call Krista came to him. To feel the sharpened ice in her voice, to hear the words between her words, the true sentiments that hid in her long pauses. This was his fault. He had lost their daughter. She was glad she'd never married him, because now he could get shipped back to Mexico once she told the police he'd never gotten his green card. He knew how to wear this ballast of guilt. Part of him yearned for it.

Instead he flipped the toggle to ON and an electric hum rose. The reels clicked to attention, the rear one full and the front one just a bare spindle. He had no clue what he was doing, but the film seemed to be threaded already, so he flipped another lever, labeled OPER. The reels spun, the tape traveled from one wheel to the next, and a blunted square of light appeared on the wall above his bed.

Blank white played out for a while, then Jandro shut the projector off. It was time to search for En. Time to repaper the neighborhood with flyers, to linger outside the police station, dredging up the courage to go inside and ask for Detective Swinson, demand some information, anything but nothing. Dreading that when he finally did, the INS would be brought up. The questions, the searching glances. Time to end up sitting inside the clown's bright head, his nose raw from the constant swipe of his army-surplus coat sleeve, waiting for two little hands to push on his shoulders, a voice to say through the giggles, "My turn, slide hog!"

Or he could empty the bottle of whiskey into the toilet, flush it into Delmar's bowels, and find some work. The thought of spending time looking for anything other than En tore at his gut. He went back to the window, stared down at those footprints leading away toward the strip of woods. "*Mija*," he whispered. He always counted on that little word to hold everything.

⁕

Jandro still held his breath every time he passed through the woods. It was his benediction for his daughter, however much he would have liked to sleep for a thousand hundred years and have En wake him with a kiss. It took barely twenty seconds to walk through the trees, motley clusters of Scotch pines, skinny birches, a few stout oaks.

When he stepped out of their shadows, letting his

breath plume out above the quilt of snow leading to the playground, he stopped. Something felt different. The town was holding its breath, too. He watched the clown's wide dinner-plate eyes, the too-small pupils. The only obvious thing was that the clouds seemed to be drifting around the little park, framing an irregular oval of sky. And the feeling, sharp and ineluctable, that he shouldn't go any farther today.

Turning around felt like a betrayal, though. Krista had said endlessly that En had probably snuck down the slide and started a game of hide and seek, waiting for Daddy to catch on. And someone else had found her, instead. Jandro just couldn't admit that those few seconds on his phone had been minutes. No one got it, how he knew En's rhythm, it was like the pulse in his blood. He still felt it, even now, pulling at him.

But he filled his lungs with the cold air, closed his mouth tight, and retreated through the trees.

*

Mr. Callum was kind enough to refer him to a job, so come morning he'd have a week's work finishing up two houses in a development out on Springer Road. Grunt work, sanding cabinets and tiling bathroom floors. Jandro capped the bitter success with a hand's worth of rye in his old Hamburglar glass, the one that always made En giggle.

He found himself orbiting the kitchen island and the projector marooned on it. Studying the knobs and switches, his eyes came back over and over to the microphone. The blank reel had no sound, of course, so he had no way of knowing if the microphone was only an odd extra speaker. But he was haunted by the insistence in Ms. Onwe's voice. The visitor in the night, or his dream of it, snapping the toggle switch up and down. Twice he nearly stepped into the hallway to knock on her door, but he was drunk and it was late.

Around midnight he hid the bottle of whiskey in the pantry. He turned the projector on, leaned close to the microphone, and whispered, "Where's my En? Tell me where she is."

He wandered over to the bed and fell across it. "Where's my little girl?" he asked again. Passing into something like sleep, he remembered he had more than a new set of kid-sized footprints to set the alarm clock for. He slept and if his dream came to him, it was too distant for him to recall, just a speck against the sky, a hawk or a precious thing called away from him in secret.

*

Jandro was grateful for the hair of the dog the next morning. After nearly two months out of work, his fingers cramped and began to blister. His knees flared with pain. He tried to pray since he was already kneeling, but it seemed God's ears had crusted over some time ago. The foreman, some guy named Franklin he'd never worked with, called him Paco all day, and near dark Jandro dragged his weighted bones onto the bus. It was snowing again. When he focused on the flakes swirling past the window it was a kind of hypnosis.

The whiskey still stood in the pantry's shadows, Jandro at his place by the window, pushing the bottle's pull. There hadn't been any footprints this morning, but it had been five a.m. when he left, and the new snow would have filled them in.

The dark tree line drew a seam across the sky, a pink echo of sun fading through empty branches. He watched and ached. He thought of the life that had been taken away from his daughter, the great puzzle of traits and decisions she would never get to be and the quirks she would never grow into. She'd hated milk—what kid ever said that? And where might that dislike have led her? Jandro remembered stealing a candy bar from Cordava's Mercado as a teenager, how Cordava himself had chased him across the street and knocked him down. He'd lost two teeth against the wall of the auto garage, which had made him too self-conscious to really smile until he'd gotten a bridge seven years later. He'd been sullen, bashful, a virgin until he was twenty-two. How much of his life, his path, his character came from that stolen Mars bar? What mistakes and the arcs of those mistakes would never be allowed to shape En?

"Buy a cheap car," he told the window and its scrim of frost. "Drive south along the Gulf, until Texas ends. Breathe the last of this air that doesn't want you. Head home to Mamá and be there when she goes."

He said these words, or something like them, every night. To taste the thought. Watching the sun bleed out, watching the purpling of the snow out on the lawn. Chasing these ghosts. "*Lo siento, mija*," he whispered. He pressed the bones around his eyes, then turned and looked at the projector. It took a moment to notice the difference. The front reel was full and the back was empty. It had been the other way around the day before, he was sure of it. A small thrill found him. He looked around the apartment, heard water coursing through the veins of someone's walls, smelled the unwashed, given-up stench that never left the air around him. He turned the projector on.

The white absence on the wall lasted only a few seconds before a deep red replaced it. Jandro switched it off in a panic, then swiped the comforter from his bed and pulled the sheet off. It was white. It would do. He rooted through his tool belt for nails and hammered them through the sheet into the drywall above the bed.

He flipped the lights off and the toggle switch back up. That deep red threw itself across the sheet, sharper now, shifting like something seen through eyelids that had just opened. A point of dark blue bled into the center, but Jandro didn't know if it was a flaw or part of the image.

Then movement, and that navy smudge came closer until it had the circumference of a poker chip. Another color intruded along its edge. He thought of a blue moon, in the first moments of eclipse by a hint of green beyond.

He found the focus dial around the lens and twisted it. The image only smeared further, so he turned it back. What he was looking at changed. The red wall rose up and he saw a strip of violet-blue sky, a ragged suggestion of treetops in the distance. His heart caught and he couldn't breathe. The view tipped forward to show a patch of sand, then two small legs in pink corduroy, two little white sneakers, and the world streamed by. Jandro felt that old rollercoaster lurch in his gut. En, on the slide. *Where's my little girl?* he'd said into the possible microphone. Her pink corduroys, her Saturday pants. On the slide.

Jandro wasn't aware of opening the door. He didn't see the hallway. The world came back to him in the rush of cold air in his ears, the crunching of snow under his work boots. The world ran with him across Adelin Street toward the trees. He gulped a huge breath at the last second before he crashed into them, dodging trunks, eyes on the field beyond. The snow cast its own ghost light at him, and somewhere off to the left static muttered. He didn't stop, hardly even thought the word *radio*.

The clown's head sat waiting for him like a cabin in a vast wilderness, as it always did, something he should never have abandoned and was lucky to return to alive. The west end of Delmar seemed distant around it, muted against the bright colors, the dejected silhouettes of the three swings, each with a rictus of snow upon its seat. It had been a sad little park, even before.

He reached the swollen purple tongue of the clown and scrabbled up the slide into the arch of its toothless mouth. It was empty. But for the deep pocket of shadow he crouched in, it was as empty as it had been the day En never came out of it.

"Virginia!" The only answer came as a soft crackle drifting from left to right to somewhere behind him. Jandro slumped down into the cold dark until he remembered the circle of sky he'd seen projected on his wall. At the apex of the clown's head, where the pyramidal angles of its red hat met, was a small hole. It framed the sky beyond in a full blue moon. He traced it with a finger, then raised himself to peer through. If there were stars, they hid behind two curtains of clouds, which bowed around the playground as they had done the previous morning.

The sky he'd seen above his bed had been a blue darkened perhaps half an hour past dusk. And that faint green, whatever it was, had partly eclipsed the hole in the plastic. There was no green now. It was past ten p.m., and Jandro wondered if he was too late, if going back to work had thrown him off course.

He'd allowed himself to think before that this playground might be a thin place between worlds, or planes. He could never share such an opaque, abstract idea with Krista, so invariably he found himself here, silent and trying to feel Virginia's hands on his shoulders.

He waited a long time because her little shove felt more possible than it ever had. She hadn't gone down the slide. Finally Jandro did—he squeezed his legs through the clown's mouth and slid down the tongue, feeling snow soak the seat of his pants.

•

Ms. Onwe didn't answer his knocks, even when they turned into pounding. Her door was locked. A voice from 2B across the hall yelled something, and Jandro gave up and went inside his apartment, where he begged the projector. He gripped its brushed-steel casing and asked the nub of microphone, "Where is she?" and a dozen variations on that theme.

He thought of calling Krista to tell her that Virginia might be trying to find him, but couldn't shape the words in a rational way. Instead he set the projector up again to finish watching, to search for clues, but the reel was now empty. The ache of his body and his strange thoughts wore him down soon after and he slept, haunted intermittently by Ens floating away from him. He counted them, reaching seventeen in the last of the dreams, until a shadow unwound onto the grass beside him, and he woke to the flapping of the projector's reel.

Someone had left the window open again. He stared through it, bleary-eyed, the tautness of the decision he had to make thrumming like a guitar string. If he ditched work he didn't know if Mr. Callum would give him another chance. He'd be consigned to the Lowe's parking lot, puffing out the chest of his thickest coat to appear stronger, more durable. There weren't many illegals in Delmar, but they still worked cheap, and he had ten years on most of them. It had been a long time since he'd had to hope his way into the bed of a pickup.

He had to leave soon to catch a bus. But the projector had filled again. He didn't know how, but his questions had been answered a second time. He imagined working all day, lost in the whine of the power sander, with the knowledge that En might be close, that there could be a key to some unknowable door—

He flipped the switch. The silent red ceiling flickered to life on the wall, and Jandro stood frozen as it played out. The sky through the hole in the clown's head was the same deep navy, but its shape was a crescent now. That out-of-focus green occluded more of the sky through the hole, pushing

161

the blue toward the edge. The image of a moon was the only one that felt right in his mind, these phases of Virginia. As before, the scene felt nothing like a film, nothing captured through a mechanical lens. It lacked a sense of defined frame, with rounded edges that felt closer to true vision.

The scene shifted, as it had yesterday, but the legs that unfolded themselves onto the slide now seemed longer and fuller through some trick of faded light, the pink corduroy stopping at the shins and tight against her legs. The purple slide a quick blur, the pale sand.

The woods shook, drawing closer. Virginia was running toward the trees. A breathless, silent trembling of the world. His body tensed with the realization that she was heading straight for him, this apartment, her weekend home, but when the trees flowed over and around the periphery, she stopped. Shapes moved, perhaps closed onto her. He couldn't pick anything out of the murk. He climbed onto the bed and tried to keep his shadow out of the projector's beam, hunched on the stripped mattress and peering up at the image like a cowed animal, but it faded white and the reel ran out behind him.

"Sand," he said. His mind had gone back to the slide. "Sand. The snow's melted. It's not time yet." He scrambled off the bed and over to the window, as though to verify that spring hadn't miraculously fallen onto the bottom corner of Delaware overnight. Through the trees across the street the sun rose with perhaps a new intensity. There were no footprints in the snow.

But the sand. He needed to wait until the snow melted and there was only sand on the playground, and the flaring hope it brought him. He went to the projector and spoke, slowly, enunciating into the microphone: "Please tell me how to get Virginia back. Please tell me when, and how. Please tell me what I need to know. *Que dios te bendiga.*" He kissed the mesh nub and grabbed his coat.

Something thumped inside Ms. Onwe's apartment as he passed in the hall. He stopped and pressed his ear to the door. A sliding, dragging sound. It could have been the old woman struggling with any of the hundreds of things she had in there.

He was already going to be late to the job site, but he knocked anyway. "Ms. Onwe?" He knocked again. "It's Jandro. I need to talk to you about your projector. Please."

There was no answer. The dragging sound had stopped. He tried the doorknob and it turned in his hand. A deep stink—gone food and mildewed laundry, worse than usual—clouded into his face as the door opened on a wedge of dark.

"Ms. Onwe?" He stepped in, pulling the collar of his army coat around his mouth. There were no lights on, and from the door he could see none of the dawn that was building outside. The brief throat of her hallway opened ahead into the close musty living room. Nothing for it except forward.

The stench deepened, became older and more complex. Heavy curtains or blankets over the single window shut the room into a tomblike black, within which his boots encountered resistance in every direction. Jandro tried to recall where he'd stepped through the hoarded junk the other day, to the lamp and projector.

"Are you home?" He listened, caught a chewing or smacking sound in front of him, something damp and suckling. Sliding to the right, he found the path, remembered the bend only when his shins knocked over a pile of magazines or newspapers. The wet sound continued and Jandro moved on. Soon his hip banged a table, and the lamp wobbled, telling him where it was. He reached down and clicked it on.

Filmy orange light puddled below, and cast in its weak glare a knot of black and white shapes moved on the floor, several feet from where he stood. He couldn't decide what he was looking at until the shapes resolved into figures, kneeling or on hands and knees, bent over something in a loose circle. Tilting the lampshade up, he threw a heavier smear of light on them. They were pressing their faces against a focal point beneath them, kissing it, their mouths making soft moans. In the stronger illumination some of the figures pushed themselves up and turned to regard him. As many as fifteen Asian males, short, and of greatly varying ages. He saw two hardly out of their teens and three stooped, withered old men. The rest were in between. They all carried a strong familial resemblance, as though several generations had gathered here for some rite, dressed in white button-up shirts and black pants with bare feet. The last few finally, grudgingly, lifted their faces to Jandro, as well. The dozens of eyes watched him. He thought of zombies, ghouls, something he could pull from a movie and plug into this, but their mouths were only drool-slicked, with no trace of blood.

And at last he saw the subject of their ardor. Ms. Onwe lay on the floor in a long powder-blue tunic. Her face shone with wetness even in the low light, and Jandro thought she was dead until her pearled eyes opened and rolled toward him. "My boys," she said. "Chun-chieh and Chih-ming, they always find me. Always love me."

The figures slowly returned to the floor and to moving their mouths over the old woman. They kissed her, extended their tongues to press against her body. "She close, Mr. Jandro," Ms. Onwe said from under them, "your daughter. Close when she left."

Jandro fled, triggering an avalanche of junk in his wake. Who in God's name were those men? What had the projector shown the old woman, and for how long? By the dirty lamplight he found the hallway and stumbled out of the apartment. He was in the street, turning toward the bus

164

stop, before he felt the difference in the air. A warmth. The sun broke through En's poisoned trees in postcard rays, and he tipped his head back to see snowmelt dripping from the building's eaves and trickling from the gutters. If it was this warm at six a.m.—

The old weight rolled over him: He forced himself again to think of his mother, go to work. All the hours before dusk had to be filled, anyway, and he could send her money in a few days. Talk to her neighbor, Lupe, find out if chemo was still an option. He felt shame, that he didn't know the answer already.

The bus drifted through slush and Jandro's mind went with it. At the unfinished house he let muscle memory guide his work, held in a vacuum of soft, pressing expectation. Every five minutes he checked a window to make sure the sun still bloomed down. It was late March. A sudden spring would not quite be a miracle, but it would be close enough for Jandro. He tried to pray, and imagined he could feel his words at last being listened to.

The snow had shrunk to gray tumors along banks and curbs by the time the crew knocked off. The sun beat like a revived heart, mid-seventies even an hour from dusk. Coming home on the bus was like waking into his dream, and it was all he could do to avoid the park. He went up to his apartment instead, hurrying past Ms. Onwe's door.

The projector had a full reel but only showed him six minutes of the ceiling of the clown's head—the square of red and the moon full. Not with blue or the blurred green of before—a mess of vague color, whitish, black, brown moved inside the circle. He went to the window. The sky lowered, draining from a richer orange to peach to yellow, then began to fill with a quick dark blue that caught him by surprise.

He ran to the stairs, down and around and out of the building, nearly colliding with Krista as he emerged onto the sidewalk. Her makeup was a ruin beneath her eyes. He had no idea she'd started wearing makeup.

"Just tell me where she is," she said, her voice thin and rising from the first word. "Tell me. I can tell Immigration it was a false alarm if you just say it."

"Immigration?" A coil of anger tightened in his chest. "You reported me? Don't talk like this, Krista. You know I don't know."

"You did something. Or you're hiding something. I've thought and thought and it's the only thing that makes sense. You—"

She shrank back from him. Jandro had never come anywhere close to striking her, through all the arguments and recent accusations. But his hand rolled into a block, and his arm tensed. He breathed. "I would never." He breathed. "Hurt our daughter." He pushed past her.

"I told them to come now," she called after him. "Where is she?" The rest of her words bled away as he crossed the street toward the woods. He filled his lungs with blessed, new spring air and pushed through.

The playground lay in an envelope of dying light when he came out of the woods, the clown's head squatting in the center. There were no clouds, so he could not discern the aperture in the sky, if it was even still there. He jogged across the patchy field, the grass bleached a sickly beige after months packed beneath the snow. But it was sand ringing the playground when he reached it, damp, with only a rind of slush along the edges.

He climbed up the slide and waited. He imagined being arrested, watching the judge hold up his deportation papers, the stern voice an atonal blur against the beating in his head. He thought of finding Virginia and being forced to leave her in the next moment. The sun seemed to sink in a final ellipse around the park, turning the west of Delmar briefly golden.

"But what did the moon mean?" he asked the night as it folded itself around him. The projector had emphasized those moons, and again he stretched up and peered through the hole in the ceiling. Nothing but the empty sky. It hit him then—the view shown by the projector had been from inside this play structure. And something had partly covered the hole. Something green. Something outside. He held up the sleeve of his drab olive coat.

He leaned out of the clown's mouth and turned himself. It was a moment's work to climb to the top of the red hat and cling there, surveying his barren little kingdom but not really seeing it. He lowered his face to the hole, slowly, thinking of the phases of the moon as his eye eclipsed it, and peeked through. And there she was. En. Her yellow coat and pink Saturday pants, her tangled dark hair.

When she saw him looking she giggled, scooted away, and shot down the slide. He heard the little squeal, the one that had been caught in the ether for nearly two months, finally release itself into the air. "Virginia!" he called, but she was off and running toward the field and the trees.

Jandro shifted to swing himself down to the sand. Something moved through the hole, inside the structure. He dipped his head again and watched another En laugh then move forward toward the clown's mouth. She was bigger now, the size of an eight-year-old. The pink corduroys were more like Capri pants, snug around her shins. Halfway across the field the first En ran with her arms up in airplane wings, teetering side to side to simulate flight.

"En!" But this second girl had already gone down the slide and was following the first. Jandro let go and braced his legs for the impact. The jolt spiked through his left ankle, which turned against the wet sand.

He set off at a limping run but then stopped. Other figures converged on this side of the playground. All female, all of them with an inexplicable yellow coat and pink pants. One little Virginia ran up to him and said, "Daddy!" as she hugged his leg. A sharp sob escaped Jandro, but she was gone before he could wrap his arms around her. A woman passed in front of him, beautiful, black-haired, with the sharp angles of Krista's face hiding under Jandro's complexion. She peered at him, narrowing her eyes. "Dad?" she said, confused, then walked toward the woods.

Jandro swiveled left, then right, taking in these fifteen, twenty daughters. A hunched old woman came up to him, with long silver-streaked hair, webs of fine wrinkles turning her face almost to paper. He saw so much of his mother in that face. For a moment she seemed on the verge of reaching out, in tenderness or for support. But she looked away shyly, then followed the others, passing another woman whose hands were laced over a belly swollen with pregnancy. His grandchild.

He thought, with a sick lurch, of the figures in Ms. Onwe's apartment. It came to him now that he had recognized those men, had seen variations of them gazing out of a dozen picture frames hanging above Ms. Onwe's hoard. Her lost sons. How far they must have come for their mother, three years across an ocean and a continent.

But these Ens did not seem profane in any way, and he understood that not only had he found En, he had found perhaps *every* En. All his possible daughters on all their possible paths, their threads of decisions, beliefs, and joys. All the ways her dots could have connected from the nexus of that morning when he lost her. It wasn't a matter of which was the real En. They all were real enough.

For a moment he could only stand and watch his girls, thankful that not one was being pulled into the sky. Off in the distance, on Milton Avenue near the municipal building, a police car's flashers burst into life, stuttering an unnatural blue into the night. Two figures emerged from the car and came toward the playground. The park was closed, Jandro told himself. Nothing to worry about. They would tell him he wasn't supposed to be here. They were regular cops. Krista hadn't really made that call.

"*La gracia de dios, Mamá,*" he murmured, "*si pudiera estar aquí,*" and followed the Virginias, the pain in his ankle forgotten. He saw another, in her late teens, whose right arm was missing at the elbow. She walked behind the others, staring down at the half-dead grass, and he quickened his pace so that he could comfort her, find out what had hurt his *mija.*

But she passed into the woods alongside the elderly Virginia. They were gone. A crackling drift of sound, either from the approaching figures behind him or as the last few rattling leaves in the trees. He plunged after his daughters, shouting their name. Black shapes stirred and came forward. The dark had grown past full, and within it arms reached out and touched him. Reunion found him. He only hoped that each one of his Ens would have the greatest blessings of life, that their sorrows would be small and their hearts full.

"Daddy," one of them whispered, then another, and another. Something was wrong with his head, a lightness and a terrible weight. He had forgotten to hold his breath. Yet all these soft arms, they stretched and embraced him there in the trees, kept him from falling, and Jandro breathed in the first moment of an eon.

Bookends

1. Certain broods of periodical cicadas emerge in either thirteen- or seventeen-year cycles. This is thought to be an evolutionary response to predation.

2. In this way, periodical cicadas, including the North American genus magicicada, *rely upon predator satiation rather than defense in order to reproduce, clawing out of the loose earth synchronously in numbers up to one and a half million per acre.*

3. They bookend Paul's time with Annie, singing as the boy first meets the girl. Years passing like water through his fingers, their offspring mourning her when it is their turn to sing from the trees.

·

The girl lay with her knees folded up toward the swollen night. "It's different when there's so many of them," she said. "They sound like everything at the same time."

The boy, just past nineteen and already half in love after the first sweet hour, watched their hands draw closer, a slow grace across the quilt laid out on the brink of the forest. He'd never met a girl so small and full of easy wonder. She couldn't have been more than five-foot-two, and he wondered how it would be to fold her against him. Too often he let his eyes take quick sips of her face, the roundness of her cheeks even when she wasn't smiling, the tight curls of her hair cropped close. His pale skin seemed to glow in the dark beside hers.

"I hear frogs," he said, thinking of the creek alongside his mother's house in Tennessee, "like the same one coming out of a million speakers."

"Or all the phones in the world calling with terrible news." She plucked at the quilt with her left hand, nearer to his hip. "But it's peaceful, somehow."

Behind them, buried in the cicada song, the clink of beer bottles and laughter. Three friends of hers, two of his, one of them mutual. The boy blessed the latter under his breath.

"Sleigh bells," he said. "Your turn."

"There's a giant refrigerator. Skyscraper big. You can hear the hum underneath."

"UFOs."

"Oh God, Paul, you're right. Don't say that." And she laughed, soft and almost a secret, a sound he would come to know better than his own. He would find himself waiting to hear it, hoping to coax it out of her.

"The emissaries have come," he said, raising his arms. She slapped his thigh above where the skin met frayed khaki, laughing again, and returned her hand to the quilt, closer still to him. He let his fingers brush against hers with the faint electricity of new touch. They stayed like that for a while. He guessed part of them never left.

.

There behind the house it should have been a peaceable dark, waking to the chirr of hidden life, the sky close and damp and wide with stars cluttered in its net. Paul stood within

172

and under it all thirteen years later, winding his courage into a tight knot before he returned to the house. He wished on those pitiless stars that somehow he could be wrong, that Annie had survived the birth. But she had not and the baby was crying again, like a wounded thing, drowning out the crickets even through the shut window.

He ignored it and leaned into the hot breath of the world, the weight of his decision. Fifteen days and he hadn't been anywhere except the cremation facility. The phone in the house was unplugged and no one took part in his bereavement.

The clay urn lay on her pillow, her ashes nestled in the space her head had made. It was cold when he reached for it in his sleep. He didn't know how to have anything but Annie. He just stood there at the mouth of the forest waiting for a sign, a music the infant could never penetrate. It had rained heavily all afternoon, cutting off the cicadas' grand performance. The grass widened into a proper field to the west, where the last of the rose siphoned from the sky. He watched the gathered trees before him, northeastward, thinking that if he walked in a straight line he would emerge from the woods, some half hour later, in the place where he and Annie had once sat on a quilt. Before either had middle names or smells or gasps in the dark.

After a time, in among the scrub pines and oaks, the first cicadas tuned up, a hesitant, searching percussion. The crickets paused as though in the knowledge they would soon be overcome. Paul listened with a bitter clarity, having waited these thirteen years to hear them again, the milestone, the circle, but now it all had broken and caught him in its quick ruin.

Behind him from the house the baby wailed its thin siren, an unending shrill thread drawn through the evening fabric. Paul had given it until tonight, its original due date. Since its mother's death had been scrubbed from its new skin, it had cried. Since he brought it home and dropped it into the crib, it had cried.

He ran his hands through his thinning hair, pulling it into vague distracted wings. His teeth clenched and he went back into the house, passing through the hallway and into the spare room. The baby's pinched screaming face was the violet of a new bruise. Paul looked down at it, his gut aching to be in here, pressed in by walls the color of muted cantaloupe, his and Annie's dreams folded away in the low antique dresser and hanging as stars and quarter moons from the speckled ceiling. He'd hung that galaxy himself. His fingers squeezed the rail of the crib they'd picked out years ago just in case Annie got pregnant. The crib was a solid piece, good dark oak, but he wished to God it was empty.

He could only stand there so long in the noise and stink, peering down at the small shape of his wife's upturned nose. Annie's eyes, too, an inexplicable meeting of brown and pale gray, though its skin was closer to the cream of his own, with only a hint of Annie's burnish. He felt one of the heavy black moments and cleared his throat, wet and ready, to spit on the baby. The verge, the tipping point, and at last he swallowed it back and fled the house wishing he could crave liquor the way some men did.

More cicadas had ratcheted into sound. Soon endless masses in crescendo, leveling off into the irrepressible monotone. Paul whispered all the things they sounded like. Washed in the tidal ocean of winding clockwork springs and burrs. He tried to make it feel like a baptism.

•

4. They live underground as nymphs for nearly all of their cycle, at depths of one to eight feet, feeding from the roots of deciduous trees along the eastern swath of the United States. On a spring evening, the signal warmth sinking down far enough into the soil, they carve exit tunnels to the surface. There they roost, immobile and entirely vulnerable, upon tree bark, porch eaves, the planks of barn walls. There is all the time in the world for them to fall prey; they have given their bodies to chance.

※

Toward the end of that first night they made a list of what the cicadas called to their minds. He used a receipt he found in his pocket, the ink long rubbed away with friction. They added *faraway screeching tires, new chalk on blackboards, rusted robot armies.* A dozen others, each more grasping than the last, wondering what the insects thought of all those years waiting in the dirt.

On the yellow rim of dawn——their friends long steeped in alcohol, slumped in beds back in the farmhouse——he looked away from her into the trees, anywhere but right at her, and almost asked her what a girl like her was doing in Blairs, with only nine hundred other folks. He'd only come for a job referral at the Mazda plant in Danville. But instead he asked if he could see her again.

"How long will these little guys be around?" She swept her arm toward the woods. They stood for a moment picking out the red-eyed cicadas coating nearby trunks like scales in the waking light.

"I can find out, if it depends on them." He turned to her now. She looked up at him and he surprised himself with a smile that felt almost sly. Sweat gleamed on their skin even at this late hour, the two of them in the humidity so long they would each look somehow different to the other the next time they met, fresh and clean.

"Better hurry. Cause if not we might have to wait until they come back." She grinned. "The return of the emissaries. Would you wait that many years for me?"

He nodded, tried to look serious. "I feel like I would."

"Then we'll see." He took her hand for a moment—as small as the rest of her, the palm almost stark white, as though his fingers were bleaching it—then let her drift into the morning. The beatific grin he'd been holding back was at last able to bloom. He heard her truck cough and grumble, listened to the crunch of gravel under the tires until the cicada song covered it all.

The two of them like the stylus of the record player they would buy in three years, lifting itself from the crackling vinyl and easing back onto the outer edge. From the start, woven into the cycle.

*

5. And so the singing. Different species each produce a characteristic call, but generally it is all considered soothing, contemplative. Many nature sound audio compilations feature cicada song.

6. The female possesses tympana, membranes stretched across a frame to detect sound. The male, alone equipped with tymbals, calls to her, muscle pushing against the hollow cavity to produce four to six thousand clicks a minute.

*

He took a shovel with him into the trees. In the overwhelming rattle of song he remembered a story Annie had told him years ago, of her parents getting lost on an island. She'd heard it equidistant in time, a year after her father died and a year before emphysema took her mother to be with him.

Her parents had honeymooned in Acadia National Park. They stood on beaches of stones shaped by eons into smooth eggs. Hiked through October forests, the violent and vast Maine colors a second ocean hissing like fire against the first.

Well before dawn on the second night, having not slept—Paul could hear Annie's laugh as she remembered how her mother blushed at this part—the newlyweds decided to climb Cadillac Mountain, from which they would be among the first few in the country to see the sunrise. A thunderstorm wrapped the island as they ascended. They sought cover in a denser part of the forest and did not find their way out of the surprising wilderness until two days later, hypothermic and weak with a bittersweet anecdote.

Nature had swallowed them. It had given them back.

The idea of losing his way even on an island soothed Paul as he loosened the earth beneath the pine straw and flung it away. He longed to be lost. But though he dug within an impressive acreage he knew where he was. The compass needle swung in his mind. He closed his eyes and spun in a slow circle with his arms held out, the shovel gripped in one fist. When he stopped, swaying like a clapper in a great bell of sound, he sensed direction. The house was now to his right, and he felt a sudden urge to check on the baby. It hadn't been fed since yesterday. He hadn't touched it since yesterday.

But he returned to his digging. The cavity deepened at the base of a tree, from the size of his wife's urn to a womb in which he might curl himself, and he imagined he could trace the tunnels the nymphs had dug on their way to the air and the light.

He wished he could see Acadia—so close to *cicada* he felt he should—hunched across Mount Desert Island, a place made of images that wouldn't fit together in his mind. Blairs, a pocket town of four sparse wooded miles, was the farthest north he'd ever been. He and Annie had often walked the length of it, never once pretending they were leaving it behind. He thought of her parents huddled beneath the old growth canopy, grains amidst the earth, telling each other they were okay, if they only walked in a straight line they'd have to come to the ocean. But how real was a memory when those who had lived it were all gone, when the only one to carry it had lost the last link in their chain?

He stopped and looked back toward the house. The baby was a part of that chain, if only an end to it. He imagined himself telling the story to it one day and his mouth went sour. The taste could have been disgust or guilt or an impotent rage. It was hard to know anymore.

He would have given anything to hear the secret laugh one last time. Annie, Annie, Annie. He called to her, his voice nothing like a song in the roar of cicadas, and listened to them repeat it, rippling out into the world in millions of waves. Knowing that even were he to see her among the trees, she would be mute, unable to answer as herself or anything on their list.

•

Other, sweeter music scored those good years in between. The cicadas became their story, their glue. When they moved into the house he found a weathered shadow box and set it on the fireplace mantel with their old scribbled receipt leaned back inside. As if it needed space to breathe.

Their jobs down in Danville, prosaic but satisfying, filled the days. She managed accounts at the bank and he made passenger doors for a hatchback coupe. They carpooled and met for park lunches. Cold nights they would play dusty records, lie pressed together on that same old quilt and plan, those plans full of little feet running through the house. For too long those plans were a few shades brighter than reality but no less considered or warm there by the fire.

On the top corners of the frame hung two cicada husks. She liked to tell him that was what he looked like before he met her.

•

7. Having left behind the brittle souvenirs of their exoskeletons, they sing and respond with little pause, continuing to embody pacifism, benign to predators and bystanders. Defense mechanisms are typically absent (see predator satiation*).*

8. They exist in the open for up to six weeks, a brief coda in such contrast to their lives within the dark soil.

                                             *

He had no stories of his own parents with which to stall his return to the house. Just more Annie moments, Annie events, all those pieces he couldn't see yet through the glaze of anger. His father was an absence, less than a ghost, and he hadn't spoken to his mother in ten years, since the afternoon when she had blurted out that, honestly and before God, Paul could do so much better than a black girl. Silence like the inside of a seashell filled the kitchen as he stared at her back, and for a minute there was only the mutter of frying eggs in the pan where she stood at the stove.

He was born a bit after the sixties, he told her. Unlike here in Knoxville (or more likely just this house), in his flat little part of Virginia there was such a thing as progress. And why hadn't she cleared the air during the past three years, even if it would only add her stink to it? Dad was as white as she was and he hadn't exactly seen him around in the past decade.

The pan had somersaulted toward him, the eggs hitting the floor and a rope of vegetable oil spattering his bare shins. He left his suitcase in the upstairs room—his old posters still on the wall, only the fresh wall calendar marking the years—and was back in Virginia before dark, pressing Annie against his chest.

                                             *

At that he wrenched shut the valve of memory, plucked a

cicada off the bark of a pine, held it close to his face. Red eyes like fish eggs, tapered bullet body under the cellophane wings. It did not move but to sing between his fingers, martyred to the fate Paul would give it. Its muffled clicks tapped like hummingbird heartbeats against his skin.

He placed it back on the tree then crushed it with the flat of his hand. It popped as he ground it against the rough bark, showing his teeth. "It's not just the baby that did it," he said. "Why couldn't she get pregnant until just before you came back?"

Soon the first tree was smeared with their innards, like weeping sap, so he moved to another. As each of the insects broke open under his palm, he thought of the birth. Two weeks early but smooth sailing, the doctor assured them, Annie's breaths coming as even and forceful as a locomotive. Until the blood. He saw it bloom on the white sheet between her legs, saw her wide eyes darting, finding him, pinning him with her dawning fear that something was wrong.

He stumbled from tree to tree. He'd stumbled into the hallway outside the delivery room, shoved out by a nurse as Annie's shouts thickened into something deeper and the doctor began barking orders. The door swung in an arc and through its weakening gaps he watched the blood. It pattered on the floor and he only thought of hot oil from a pan here, now, hammering his fists at the impossible numbers of cicadas, the patient emissaries. He did not know if he was prey or predator, for they sang on without acknowledging his presence.

The faithful compass led him right into his own yard, the house looming, the baby's cries finding every crack in the walls and sills and leaking out to him. The shovel fell from his hand. "I have to feed it first," he said, and didn't recognize his own voice through his hoarse sobs. "I have to feed it, at least." But he passed through the kitchen into the living room, where he grabbed the shadow box from the mantel and hurled it into a wall. A cicada husk landed in front of him and he relished the dry crunch of it under his boot.

He turned back to the kitchen but stopped, looking down at the quilt spread out on the floor, waiting. He wadded it into a checkered ball and stood squeezing it, looking down the hall toward the spare room.

For a long moment he considered leaving the hole he'd made in the forest an open wound. He could strap the baby in the carrier, the tags still hanging from its handle, and drive the six hours to Knoxville. Leave it on the doorstep so its grandmother would bear the fruits of her bigotry. But he pictured the blood pooling on the shining tiles of the delivery room floor as the door sighed toward and away from him. His arms too numb to even reach out and push it.

He walked down the hall and stood in the guest room doorway, watching the wailing silhouette in the crib. The smell of it clouded the air with rank sweetness. He went into the room, arms lifted, and the quilt eclipsed the baby. Better if he couldn't see. When he pressed the quilt down over it, a blessed silence resounded until the cicada song crept into the room. He tried to bare his teeth again but couldn't.

There was not enough life in it yet to struggle. But the muscles in his arms strained as though wrestling a feral thing. Could he blame it for wanting to be born, even as it left the husk of its mother behind? Could he blame the cicadas for the same blind need? He carried this blame with him, a thing of such grave weight, as if to fit it into every mold to find where it belonged.

He lifted the quilt away, for a moment certain it was dead. His heart stuttered and fought to regain its rhythm. When the baby's face twisted and the cries burst out of it louder than before, he wept with a relief that awed him.

He should feed it first. Wash it. He owed that much to the future he and Annie were supposed to have.

·

9. But in that coda they, like all things, live so that their young may live. They have tapped into the slow vein of evolution for their young. It is why the male sings. It is why the female listens to the words.

·

After the bottle of formula was gone he ran an inch of warm water in the tub and laid the baby down, cupping a hand behind the soft down of its head. Its cries were reedy, magnified in the tiled space. One by one, stained washcloths filled the small wire trashcan beside the sink. His cheeks burned with shame at the angry rash coating the insides of its legs, at the clotted brown bathwater swirling down the drain. He wrapped the baby in a towel and sat on the toilet, patting it dry. "Her," he said. She lay across his lap, curling her fingers. "She." One of his eyes was visible in the bottom corner of the mirror. He returned its stare for a long time, thinking of links in chains.

He came out of the bathroom, the baby clean and soft and fitted into the crook of his arm. She had fallen into silence, her eyes closed. He looked through the picture window, where the trees were indistinct as the filth clouding the bathwater. "What am I supposed to do?" he asked.

The cicada song was muted inside the house but still persistently there. He focused on the open hum underneath. Did they long for light all those years, of air to hold their song? "I would have to give you a name," he said, lifting the baby so that her smell filled his nostrils. Soap and something else he couldn't name. Annie had refused to trade suggestions for names; she insisted on waiting until she saw their daughter for the first time. The baby would name herself in that moment. One word, Alina, opened in his mind like petals. It was a nice name, he thought. Annie would love it, would say it had a little of both of them in it. But he couldn't bring himself to pronounce it, feel the wings of it in his mouth before setting it loose.

"What am I supposed to do?" he said again. His lips touched the curve of her forehead. He left them there, humming a refrain that was part melody and part memory. His mouth against her fresh raw skin, he felt his own semblance of song vibrate against his teeth. He tried to imagine keeping the baby for thirteen years, tried to picture her in some far morning, the very first to see the sunrise glance around the rim of the world. Finally he looked up and out the window, said into the green darkness, "I could do that. Then they'll come back. Then we'll see."

*

10. In the minutes after molting their wings inflate. The white bodies soon darken with life.

Story Notes

"Beside Me Singing in the Wilderness" This story won a contest held by Shock Totem Publications, in which authors were given a week to write about a bleeding mountain. I imagined two little girls living in the dark, both in terms of environment and in terms of their understanding of it. When they come out of the dark, it is still in their veins. I let Alma and Sissa's affliction veer quite close to vampire territory while keeping the line trailing back into the bowels of that mountain and whatever ancient thing might dwell there, but the theme I wanted to explore with this story was only: What if you'd been made a monster but didn't know why? Would you go on? Would you give in? And what would the price be of staying true?

I'd also been wanting to write in a thick southern vernacular. It was like coming home.

"Onanon" I kept thinking about infected text, the idea that words on a page could carry an occult intent. A living document, so to speak. Poor, untethered Adam doesn't know what to trust in his own life, and the explanation itself doesn't make things any easier. Even the title, "Onanon," is a piece of gibberish that almost makes sense, and once it was rooted in my mind, something had to be done with it.

Or I could claim it was Lovecraft by way of bees. The elder queen, so to speak. There's very little that scares me in this world, but from a very early age I was terrified of bees, hornets, and wasps. Those flying, stinging creatures. Bees have an elegance the others do not, however, and that old hive hanging in the mountain cabin, along with all the mythology that might have once dripped from it, was a vivid image within which "Onanon" honeycombed.

"Greener Pastures" I sort of wanted to write a *Twilight Zone* episode, but also something with strict parameters that *Alfred Hitchcock Presents* might have appreciated. I gave myself one setting and one brief, fluid time frame and wrote "Greener Pastures." I thought of this story as my mini-cosmic horror piece, and that could still hold true at only 3,000 words, but it took on a life of its own and seemed a bit angry at me for slapping the label "mini" on it.

America is nothing without its interstates, and the interstates are nothing without their truckers. That lonely job still has a sort of sad romance about it, from the language of the CB radio to the drone of all those wheels on the highways. The same sodium lights on a loop, on an endless strip. Although the trucking industry is still very much alive, it often feels like truckers are a relic of the past, and the blank spaces on the maps have less traffic in them. The rest stops and all-night diners tucked into these spaces feel more lonesome. I wanted to write about them in a sort of anti-ghost story. We are all haunted by our dead—it is a motif that has been and always will be a resonant voice. But what if the voice is that of the living? Truckers leave behind their loved ones for long stretches at a time, and there is a lot of empty road out there before the dawn.

"A Discreet Music" When Simon Strantzas asked me to

write a story for an anthology he was editing, I was floored. When he told me it was a tribute to Robert Aickman, I was nervous. Not only is Aickman one of my favorite authors, he is a singular author. His stories follow their own interior logic while never drifting too far from the beaten path into experimental surrealism or some other sub-sub-category. The most obtuse Aickman tale still has the ability to shock, creep out, and stick in the mind. An intimidating writer to pay homage to.

Strantzas wanted us authors to pay tribute to Aickman based on our own personal worldview and fiction, tapping into how Aickman's work had changed its weave. I chose to open my story with a very un-Aickman image—a man beginning to turn into a swan—and see how I thought Aickman would have handled a Kafka or Borges conceit. That was the idea, anyway, a sort of challenge.

The title of the story comes from Brian Eno's 1975 album, *Discreet Music*, which was famously conceived while he convalesced following an accident and couldn't get out of the hospital bed to turn up the classical music that was softly playing. The low volume began to become a crucial character of the music itself, and this would go a long way toward Eno's role in birthing the ambient music genre. The insinuation, the mystery, the lure—this discreet music scored Hiram's mourning and rebirth, as he came to terms with the loss of his wife and what it meant for another love he had never followed. When Hiram's own bones are mending, one can easily see how I lifted the inspiration straight from this record's origin story.

As the Yeats epigraph makes clear, the story also owes a great debt to "Leda and the Swan." Although as to what name Hiram's new companion gives there at the end, by the water, it might not be so easy as that. Another layer of the onion, another attempt to honor Aickman's wonderful, elusive body of work.

"The Devil Under the Maison Blue" There was this image I couldn't shake: a girl sitting on top of a tall house. It seemed so lonely, and it was deep into fall with the birds almost gone. What drove her up there to such a dangerous height? I hoped she'd done it enough times to have a sure sense of balance, though she clearly did not have a sure sense of place. I began to realize that the answer to her presence up there was difficult, and uncomfortable. But that's what I'm supposed to do, right? Stare into the face of such things.

As for Mr. Elling, he had a story of his own to tell. The dynamic between him and Gillian—such different people with subtly kindred spirits and not so subtly vile fathers—seemed to be an opportunity to explore the Faustian bargain. And I wanted to inhale the dust of jazz through it. I find it strange that of all the fiction I've written, I feel most connected to Mr. Elling's voice. I have virtually nothing in common with him and couldn't possibly relate to his life. But Gillian was able to, in a way. And this was me trying to as well.

"October Film Haunt: *Under the House*" And, inevitably, the found-footage film genre. I'm still a sucker for it when it's done well, so of course I had to try my hand at it. But I don't get to use visuals here, outside of Michael Bukowski's amazing depiction of the golden shepherd on the cover of this book. So I thought about what it would be like if a bunch of aspiring horror authors tried to "shoot" a documentary using only words, essentially recording events and observations in a round-robin context.

Clearly there's a bit of *The Blair Witch Project* woven into this story. And a love of the epistolary style of pasting Web pages into a narrative and peppering things with a bit of Reddit and YouTube. But as effective as the "journal" trope can still be, I wanted to force my doomed characters into a detached mode, as though they were behind a camera. I had a lot of fun with the way that particular mode unravels, the failure of a removed narrative. And once it does, the camera has no choice but to come out, and I finally got to write in night vision.

"Deducted From Your Share in Paradise" Another story that began with a wordless image, just women falling from the sky, silhouetted against the setting sun, their black dresses fluttering. There was silence, a great dust bowl of silence, a sad forgotten trailer park as more images began to click in, and I heard their bodies hitting the ground, impacting the roofs of the trailers.

Were they angels fallen from heaven? I wasn't sure, so I tried to find out. But what drew my mind more fiercely turned out to be how the residents of the trailer park treated these strange visitors, how people in power use those beneath them, and the used in turn use others. No, these aren't all innocent people against whom dark forces are working. And those old tables turned into what the women needed from them to get home. I chose a boy to see all this through, because I find I don't write from the perspective of youth enough. The innocence that hasn't been torn away quite yet. Maybe it's because the nostalgia is somehow still too raw, at times. In any event, this little commune in the parched Texas nowhere undergoes quite the change. The only question is which god has been listening to their prayers.

"The Inconsolable" A breakup is a lonely thing. Not only because of the relationship that has ended but also because it can feel, to the bereft, like those around you don't see it as a true *loss*. No one has died. You shouldn't really even be using that word *bereft*. You're supposed to move on. You're supposed to be a grownup. Sometimes, though, it's not that simple. In a strange way, the pain of loss can be stronger because what you've lost *is* still out there, breathing, laughing, blushing at someone else's words. And sometimes a part of *you* has maybe died, and it's not your fault that you feel these things the way you do.

This story started as nothing more than a title. "The Inconsolable." That definite article seemed to hold a lot of power in it. Growing up I was haunted by the ubiquitous (at least in the Bible Belt) little poem "Footprints in the Sand" and the difficulty of faith. It came to me strongly when I was beginning this story, and I thought about how so many turn to God in their darkest hour. There is such powerful comfort. Faith is a blind thing, you're not even supposed to understand it, so it wouldn't be surprising, in a horror context, if there's some fine print.

"Dancers" This is another story where I attempted to walk around the edges of cosmic horror. Cthulhu need not be summoned from a forbidden tome, or through the rites of an arcane cult offering ancient knowledge. In a small town, in the lives of regular people, cosmic horror could infiltrate in any number of ways. I riffed off of demonic possession because there are many in America that would interpret a Lovecraftian sort of mythos through a Christian lens. And trees figure into my work probably more than any other element, so I found myself writing a story starring two interesting ones.

But what I really wanted to do here was examine a marriage. How it grows and how it rots, both when it is properly maintained and when it is not. And how the question of having children can affect its root system over the course of many years. See, there I go with the trees again.

"A Thousand Hundred Years" Another atavistic fear: In the space of a few moments, your child has vanished. In the mall, on the playground, everything you hold dear and as a sense of rightness in the world can be taken away from you.

Here I wanted to look at a situation where no one would believe the father because the playground was deserted. His story simply couldn't add up. And as an immigrant, distrust and suspicion would fall even harder upon him, all while crushing guilt pulled at him from two different countries.

I was fascinated by the idea of all the possible versions of a child that could have sprung from that fateful moment, all the mistakes and victories and choices that had been snuffed out. A loss is not just a linear, present-tense thing. This was where the story really began to tell itself, through Jandro's anguish, his relentless pursuit and faith.

"Bookends" I believe I will always write about loss. Is there a greater fear? Thus far I have escaped the deepest of losses, but I know this fortune will one day have to end. And then I will write about it from the well of experience.

"Bookends" started in my mind as a man standing in his back yard as a vast chorus of cicadas rose with idiot grace. Behind him, ignored inside the house, a baby wailed. I didn't have to peer too closely into that dark to see what caused this painful scene. I knew that the man's wife had died in childbirth, and that the man could not bring himself to be a father because he blamed the baby for his loss. The place his thoughts were going to—I had to know what he would do in that place.

This is the only story in this collection that does not feature the supernatural in some way. I let the story push up against the possibility of the other, but it asked that it remain a horror that is very real, and very simple. And it asked that it conclude with a glimmer of hope in its bleak dark, because none of these stories, including the ones that end in doom and terror, are anything without the ability to hope. And with that reality, with that bit of bright maybe, I felt it best that "Bookends" said our goodbyes.

Acknowledgments

You only get one first book, and so I feel the urge to thank nearly everyone I've ever met. The horror and weird fiction community is a nurturing one, an enthusiastic and supportive one. My friends and family even more so.

But to keep it to a readable length, I must shine a light on: David G. Blake, Samuel Marzioli, Kristi DeMeester, John Boden, K. Allen Wood, Evan Dicken, Michael Kelly, Paula Guran, Sean Wallace, Anya Martin, Scott Nicolay, Michael Bukowski, Justin Steele, Joe Pulver, Matthew M. Bartlett, Mike Griffin, John Guzman, S.J. Bagley, Silvia Moreno-Garcia, John Claude Smith, Kurt Fawver, Usman T. Malik, Chris Power, Bobby Power, Robyn Power, Christian Sager, Robert Lamb, Philip Fracassi, Audie Timms, CM Muller, Art Vuley, all the wonderful Vuleys, Chris Riley, Josh Avren, Alex Morgan, Farbod Kokabi, David Surface, Abbey Meaker, Laird Barron, Peggy Corbett (the best AP English teacher anyone could ask for), Sam Cowan, John Eubanks. I've forgotten some of you, I know. There's no way I couldn't. But you are all lovely.

Gratitude to Simon Strantzas, for writing my introduction

and providing valuable insight into the business of being a real live author. Vast thanks, for reading the stories and telling the world things about them that made my decade: Steve Rasnic Tem, Gemma Files, Richard Gavin, Damien Angelica Walters, Brian Evenson, S.P. Miskowski, John Langan, Paul Tremblay, David Nickle, Bracken MacLeod, Nathan Ballingrud.

My parents, Kathleen and Larry, are such beautiful people. My brothers. My aunt June and all the branches of the Wehunt and Edge trees.

And finally my partner, Natalia, who is close to half the reason these stories exist. She was the one who couldn't understand why I hadn't yet followed the dream into the forest. She was the one who wanted me to, with a hand pressing at my back. It's been wonderful getting lost in all these pines with her by my side.

About the Author

MICHAEL WEHUNT grew up in North Georgia, close enough to the Appalachians to feel them but not quite easily see them. There were woods, and woodsmoke, and warmth. He did not make it far when he left, falling sixty miles south to the lost city of Atlanta, where there are fewer woods but still many trees. He lives with his partner and his dog and too many books, among which Robert Aickman fidgets next to Flannery O'Connor on his favorite bookshelf.

His fiction has appeared in various places, such as *The Year's Best Dark Fantasy & Horror*, *The Year's Best Weird Fiction*, and *The Mammoth Book of Cthulhu*. This is his first collection.

About the Artist

MICHAEL BUKOWSKI has been a freelance illustrator for 15 years, mostly working for punk and metal bands across the world. However, in 2011 he started working on the *Illustro Obscurum* project in which he is illustrating every creature/god in the fiction of author H.P. Lovecraft. More recently he's been illustrating creatures from other prominent horror and weird fiction authors past and present.

Michael lives in Philadelphia with his partner, the painter Jeanne D'Angelo, and their three annoying cats. He loves horror movies, vegetarian food and traveling the world to see dead stuff on public display.

Also Available from
SHOCK TOTEM PUBLICATIONS

CURIOUS TALES *of the* MACABRE *and* TWISTED

SHOCK TOTEM

T.L. Morganfield
Kurt Newton • Don D'Ammassa
Jennifer Pelland • David Niall Wilson
Conversations with John Skipp, William Ollie, and Alan Robert

SHOCK TOTEM MAGAZINE
Issue #1 – July 2009

CURIOUS TALES *of the* MACABRE *and* TWISTED

SHOCK TOTEM

LESLIANNE WILDER
RICARDO BARE • CATE GARDNER
VINCENT PENDERGAST • DAVID JACK BELL
GRÁ LINNAEA & SARAH DUNN
A conversation with James Newman • Non-fiction by Mercedes M. Yardley

SHOCK TOTEM MAGAZINE
Issue #2 – July 2010

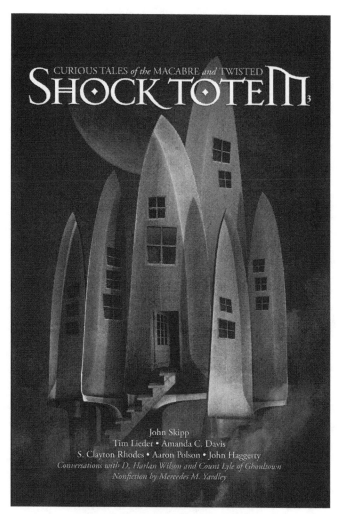

CURIOUS TALES *of the* MACABRE *and* TWISTED

SHOCK TOTEM₃

John Skipp
Tim Lieder • Amanda C. Davis
S. Clayton Rhodes • Aaron Polson • John Haggerty
Conversations with D. Harlan Wilson and Count Lyle of Ghoultown
Nonfiction by Mercedes M. Yardley

SHOCK TOTEM MAGAZINE
Issue #3 – January 2011

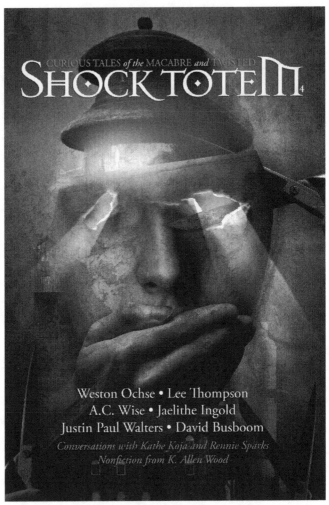

CURIOUS TALES *of the* MACABRE *and* TWISTED

SHOCK TOTEM 4

Weston Ochse • Lee Thompson
A.C. Wise • Jaelithe Ingold
Justin Paul Walters • David Busboom
Conversations with Kathe Koja and Rennie Sparks
Nonfiction from K. Allen Wood

SHOCK TOTEM MAGAZINE
Issue #4 – July 2011

HOLIDAY TALES *of the* MACABRE *and* TWISTED

SHOCK TOTEM

Christmas 2011

Kevin J. Anderson • K. Allen Wood • Mercedes M. Yardley
Robert J. Duperre • John Boden • Ryan Bridger
Nick Contor • Sarah Wood

*Holiday Recollections from Jack Ketchum, Mark Allan Gunnells, Lee Thompson,
Leslianne Wilder, Jennifer Pelland, Nick Cato, and more...*

SHOCK TOTEM MAGAZINE
Special Holiday Issue – Christmas 2011

CURIOUS TALES *of the* MACABRE *and* TWISTED

SHOCK TOTEM₅

Ari Marmell • Darrell Schweitzer
Kurt Newton • Joe Mirabello • Sean Eads
Mekenzie Larsen • Jaelithe Ingold
A Conversation with Jack Ketchum • Nonfiction from Nick Contor

SHOCK TOTEM MAGAZINE
Issue #5 – July 2012

CURIOUS TALES *of the* MACABRE *and* TWISTED

SHOCK TOTEM 6

Jack Ketchum • Lee Thompson
Michael Wehunt • Lucia Starkey • P.K. Gardner
Addison Clift • Hubert Dade
Conversation with Lee Thompson • Nonfiction from John Boden

SHOCK TOTEM MAGAZINE
Issue #6 – January 2013

CURIOUS TALES *of the* MACABRE *and* TWISTED

SHOCK TOTEM ₇

William F. Nolan • S. Clayton Rhodes
Amberle L. Husbands • Kristi DeMeester • M. Bennardo
Damien Angelica Walters • Victoria Jakes
Conversations with Laird Barron and Violet LeVoit
Nonfiction from Kurt Newton

SHOCK TOTEM MAGAZINE
Issue #7 – July 2013

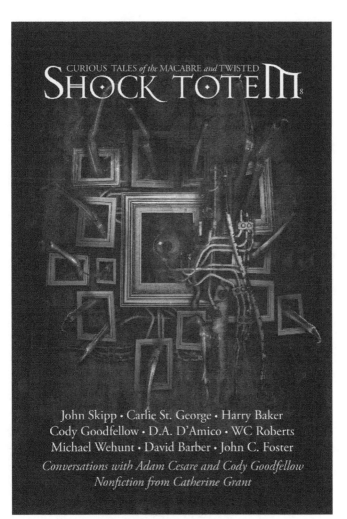

CURIOUS TALES *of the* MACABRE *and* TWISTED

SHOCK TOTEM 8

John Skipp • Carlie St. George • Harry Baker
Cody Goodfellow • D.A. D'Amico • WC Roberts
Michael Wehunt • David Barber • John C. Foster
Conversations with Adam Cesare and Cody Goodfellow
Nonfiction from Catherine Grant

SHOCK TOTEM MAGAZINE
Issue #8 – January 2014

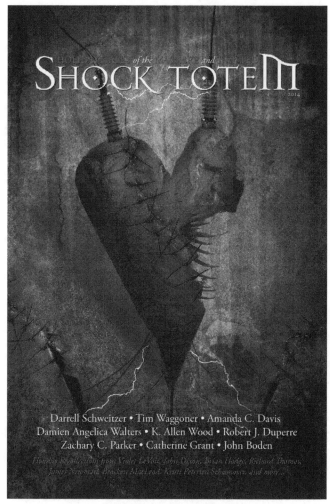

SHOCK TOTEM MAGAZINE

Special Holiday Issue – Valentine's Day 2014

CURIOUS TALES of the MACABRE and TWISTED

SHOCK TOTEM

Stephen Graham Jones • Bracken MacLeod • Emma Osborne
Karen Runge • Kathryn Ohnaka • S.R. Mastrantone
Peter Gutierrez • Evan Dicken • Tim Lieder
Conversations with F. Paul Wilson and Stephen Graham Jones
Nonfiction by Catherine Grant

SHOCK TOTEM MAGAZINE
Issue #9 – July 2014

HOLIDAY TALES *of the* MACABRE *and* TWISTED

SHOCK TOTEM

HALLOWEEN 2014

Sydney Leigh • David G. Blake • Kriscinda Lee Everitt
K. Allen Wood • John Boden and Bracken MacLeod
Kevin Lucia • Rose Blackthorn • Barry Lee Dejasu

Holiday Recollections from John Langan, Jeremy Wagner, Lee Thomas,
Mike Lombardo, and Babs Boden

SHOCK TOTEM MAGAZINE
Special Holiday Issue – Halloween 2014

CURIOUS TALES *of the* MACABRE *and* TWISTED

SHOCK TOTEM₁₀

Samuel Marzioli • David G. Blake • Trace Conger
Mary Pletsch • Thana Niveau • Sarah L. Johnson
Leslie J. Anderson • Paul Andrew Hamilton • D.K. Wayrd

Conversations with T.E.D. Klein and Paul Tremblay
Nonfiction from K. Allen Wood

SHOCK TOTEM MAGAZINE
Issue #10 – July 2015

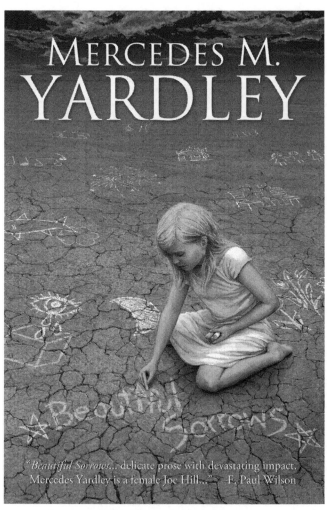

"*Beautiful Sorrows*... delicate prose with devastating impact. Mercedes Yardley is a female Joe Hill..." —F. Paul Wilson

BEAUTIFUL SORROWS

MERCEDES M. YARDLEY

FROM HELL HE COMES...

AND HE WANTS THE CHILDREN

THE WICKED

A NOVEL OF UNHOLY TERROR BY

JAMES NEWMAN

THE WICKED

JAMES NEWMAN

"*Ugly As Sin*...is the most jaundiced indictment possible of the corrupted soul of celebrity culture...its feeders and especially its fed." —Brian Hodge

UGLY AS SIN

A Novel of White-Trash Noir by

JAMES NEWMAN

UGLY AS SIN
JAMES NEWMAN

ZERO LIVES REMAINING
ADAM CESARE

DOMINOES

JOHN BODEN

Find Us Online

http://www.shocktotem.com
http://www.twitter.com/shocktotem
http://www.facebook.com/shocktotem
http://www.youtube.com/shocktotemmag

Made in the USA
San Bernardino, CA
11 November 2016